PSHE

DENNY
and the Magic Pool

Pamela Purnell

PONT BOOKS

First Impression—1993
Second Impression—February 1995
Third Impression—March 1999
Fourth Impression—June 2000

ISBN 0 86383 990 8

This volume is published with the support of the Welsh Arts Council.

Printed by
J. D. Lewis & Sons Ltd., Gomer Press, Llandysul, Ceredigion

For my friends at Thornwell Road Junior School
and for my brother, Calvin,
who loved to go "over the tide".

1

Denny banged his knuckles hard, rapping on Nana's front door. It glistened, sleek with bright yellow paint, matching the single flat window frame. Nana's hobby was choosing new shades of super-gloss to keep her little house looking smart and tidy but Denny was too cold to admire it at that moment.

'Hurry up . . . hurry up . . .' Denny stamped his feet, muttering through tight lips. The ice-white net curtain moved and then Nana opened the door. She didn't seem surprised to see him.

'I thought it must be you, our Denny! Come in— you look frozen. You haven't had your tea, love?'

'No. Mam's not home.' He darted in and slammed the door, shutting out the cold. Nana walked ahead of him back to her kitchen. Denny followed down the narrow passage, touching the clean, crisp wallpaper as he went.

Nana put another knife and fork and a glass tumbler on the embroidered table-cloth. Denny eyed the round chocolate cake, rich and tempting.

'Egg on toast first!' Nana smiled fondly at him.

'Ooh, yeah! Thanks. Nana . . . where's my Mam gone?'

Nana turned to the stove. 'Don't worry, love. She told me she might be late today. She won't be long. Do you want to watch the telly or just talk?'

'Talk, if you like.' Denny could do both, watch and talk, at the same time but Nana didn't like competition when she was chatting. Her television set stood on a shelf in the corner of the kitchen. Nana put it on when she was sewing. 'A bit of life,' she called it. Nana sewed a lot. From open-air market stalls she collected fat bundles of cut-price fabrics and turned them into smart clothes. Her electric zig-zag machine, now resting with a cloth over it, sewed miles in minutes.

Denny looked at her. Nana was said to be amazing for her age. A few called her 'mutton dressed as lamb' but Denny's Mam said they were jealous. Nana was wearing tight blue trousers and a vivid red and yellow flowered shirt. Her elegant little feet were strapped into dainty high-heeled sandals and the sheen of her platinum hair swung silky and loose about her trim shoulders. Nana had stayed looking young although, of course, she was as old as the hills. Well, that's what she said.

Denny took off his jacket and scarf and washed his hands at the kitchen sink. The house had an even cosiness so that there was no need to huddle up over the fire. Denny liked having tea at Nana's. She gave him Coca-Cola to drink with his food, a treat he didn't get at home. He sat at the table, waiting while the eggs poached gently and Nana slipped bread slices in the toaster. In a few minutes, Nana put a loaded plate in front of him. He pierced the eggs and the yolks oozed as sunny yellow as Nana's front door.

'There's a good boy, then! Eat up, love.'

Nana sat in her place opposite him and poured tea into her cup. Her fingers, daintily handling the little bone-china teapot, were tipped with soft pink nail colour. Nana 'kept herself nice'—as nice as she kept her terraced house in Owen Street. Denny's relations had lived in the lower part of Cardiff for generations, working at labouring and cleaning jobs and bringing up families in the crowded, decaying streets. The area was shabby and grander parts of the city looked down on it but around every corner were familiar faces and busy untidy little shops. Warm, friendly . . . It was Denny's world.

Denny's eggs and toast disappeared swiftly and he was ready for the cake. He took large bites of the generous helping Nana cut for him and washed it down with the dark fizz.

'More, love?'

Denny nodded. 'Yes please, Nana.' She refilled his glass and cut into the cake again, her eyes happy. 'You're a lovely boy! Nana's angel!'

Denny was embarrassed when Nana talked soft like that. Still, his mates weren't there to hear her so he suffered it and savoured his second piece of cake, eating more slowly now, his first desperate hunger satisfied.

'Your Mam won't be very late. She's gone to see about a job.'

Denny knew that it wasn't easy for his mother, managing alone since his dad left. She had been looking for a job for months.

'Will my Dad come back, Nana?'

Nana didn't answer straight away. She sipped tea and then said, 'It's no use pretending. You're big enough to understand. Your Mam and Dad have split up really serious this time. I heard he's gone to London.'

Denny gazed down at his plate, his bottom teeth dragging at his top lip.

'Ay—you still look hungry!' Nana said quickly. She opened a couple of tins and put a bowl of pears and rice-pudding before Denny. He spooned up the blend, sharp and sweet on his tongue.

'You see, Denny love,' said Nana, sitting down again, 'grown-ups make mistakes. They're not perfect. When they get married they make vows and promises—then there's a big party with champagne and flowers—they want to live happy-ever-after. And some do.' Her voice lowered. 'But not everybody. For some people it goes wrong.'

Denny looked at her, his blue eyes wide. He felt scared, a cold tingle creeping about in his body. He remembered the shouting and crashing in the flat and himself being hastily rushed around to Nana's. His mother had cried non-stop.

'Always short of money, that was their downfall. Bad managers the pair of them.' Nana sighed. On her sideboard was a wedding picture of Denny's Mam and Dad. His father dark and handsome, his mother doll-pretty with a white frothy thing on her head. They laughed at the camera in a swirl of confetti.

'Yes—well—it doesn't always work out, love. Never mind. We've got *you*—so something good came of it!' Denny scraped his bowl carefully. He would always be part Mam, part Dad. Nobody could ever take that away from him.

Nana brightened. She had a quick, changeable way with her, able to shake off gloom in a second.

'Let's have a bit of light on the subject!' she said, going to the wall switch. 'The nights are closing in.'

The sudden glare revealed Nana's smooth unlined face, rosied by the warmth of the room. She continued to take his mind off family troubles. She scrunched up her shoulders and wrinkled her nose, a funny habit of hers when she was planning something nice.

'It's your birthday in a few weeks. Ten! There'll be something special for a lovely boy!'

Denny knew that the playful baby-talk was to cheer him up, try to make him forget his worries and it was a chance not to be missed.

'Skates, Nana? Can I have roller-skates?'

She pulled another funny face. 'We'll see. I'll have to save my pennies.'

Denny relaxed, certain then that the skates were his. She would have tried to influence his choice, otherwise. Nana took care of him too well, in a way. Other kids, even the little ones, had skates ages ago while he was told to wait. Apparently, on the stroke of ten years old he could be trusted not to break his neck or cannon into the traffic. Secretly though, unknown to Nana or Mam, he was a skilled skater already. On borrowed wheels he had been practising down the side lanes for years. They'd be amazed at how quickly he would learn.

After tea, Nana said—'Your Mam will call here for you, love. That new pop programme is on in a minute.' This was her way of stopping him going out. She disapproved of Denny traipsing the streets when it was getting dark.

Nana wasn't the grumpy kind, though. She enjoyed lively programmes with plenty of bright colours. When the first group came on the screen, she danced around the kitchen to the heavy beat. Nana was a great mover. Denny grinned.

'Come on, our Den!'

So Denny tried out a routine he'd picked up at the school disco. Bend—twist—twist—bend—kick and back—kick and back . . .

'Smashing, Den!' cried Nana, shaking her hips in the tight pants.

The music blared and roared and thumped, the telly images gyrated and flashed over the screen.

Denny and Nana threw themselves into their own private disco . . .

The metallic hammering of the front door knocker went almost unheard. 'Listen!' said Nana, stopping. Denny turned down the volume.

'Oo eck! That'll be your Mam,' said Nana.

'Cup of tea, Trish?'

Mam sat in Nana's kitchen without taking off her coat. She might have been an older and poorer sister of the bride in the photograph. The brownish, greasy growth of her hair pushed out the dry blonde perm and her face was pinched with cold and anxiety, pale except for her post-box red mouth and blushered cheeks. Black stuff ringed her bitter brown eyes like the markings of a strange, startled bird. Denny looked away. He wondered why his mother took so much trouble to spoil her good looks.

'Thanks, Mam. I'd love a cuppa. I'm perished.'

Nana was her mother and 'Mam' to her. Denny found it hard to believe that she had once been a little girl, born and brought up in this house. He watched his mother light a cigarette. Nana hated anyone smoking in her home but she said nothing. She handed over the cup of tea and Denny's Mam took it, hands trembling.

'What you been up to, then?' his Mam snapped at him.

'Nothin'!' Denny was peeved and defensive.

'Came straight round here, did you?'

'Yes! If I can't get in at home, I have to come to Nana's. I'm not stupid.' His voice was edgy, aggressive. His Mam knew that hunger would drive him to his grandmother if not obedience.

'H'm.' His mother gave him a suspicious, narrow-eyed stare.

Nana put her arm about Denny's shoulders. 'He's a good boy, Trish. Don't pick on him the minute you see him.'

Denny hated being attacked and protected by the two women. He wriggled away from Nana.

Nana asked—'Well, did you get the job?'

Denny's Mam sucked in smoke and blew it out into the room.

'No. It was taken. Waitress, that was. Evenings only. No—the one I was offered is a bit different.'

Denny pretended to watch the almost silent screen.

'It's a live-in job at one of the new hotels outside Newport. Chambermaid to start with but I could go on to better things.'

'Good money?'

'Not bad—and I'll get my keep. Only—' Denny's Mam glanced over at him. 'There's you-know-who to think of.'

Nana said quietly—'Turn off that telly, love. Did you hear what your Mam said?'

14

Denny pressed the standby button and the television screen dissolved to a central dot.

'Yeah. I heard. She's goin' away to work.'

'Don't look as if it's a crime!' his mother complained. 'I'm trying to do my best.'

'Of course you are, Trish. Your Mam's a bit upset, Denny. Now listen to me, both of you . . .'

Nana arranged matters calmly. She brought Denny into the discussion, asking his opinion so often that most of his anger and resentment faded.

'So that's settled,' Nana said. 'Denny will live here with me. You'll get time off to come home, Trish, so you'll see each other often.'

'I'll be able to send you money,' his mother told Nana.

'See how you go. We'll manage—won't we, Den?' Nan smiled at him. 'We'll be company for each other.'

'Yeah. Yeah—we'll manage.'

His mother stood up, belting her short leather coat tightly over her mini-skirt. 'You behave yourself, then, and help your Nana. And don't be cheeky.'

'He's never cheeky! He's a lovely old kid. Now what about his things?'

At the door his mother said—'I'll clear out the flat over the weekend. Come on over when you have a minute. Can he stay here tonight?'

'Yes! You'd like that, wouldn't you, Den?'

He tried to look unconcerned. 'Yeah. Suppose so. See you, Mam.' Nana kept spare pyjamas for him in case of emergencies. He'd worn them a lot recently.

Later, he went upstairs to what Nana called 'Denny's room.' A home from home. He'd stayed there for years when his parents went out for an evening or when he fell asleep and had grown too heavy to be carried home to the flat. Nana kept the bed clean and aired, ready for him at any time. He sat on it, his arms slack at his sides. The full shock hit him. He had lost his Mam and Dad in the space of a few months. He recalled something similar from a book or a film. Losing one parent was unfortunate; losing two was careless. Denny thought that it was meant to be a joke but he failed to see anything funny in it. Despite the comfort of the warm, spotless little house he felt chilled and desolate.

He undressed and got into bed. Nana loves you . . . Nana loves you . . . repeated in his head. And Nana came in to snuggle him down like when he was little and brought him a mug of cocoa to give him sweet dreams . . . yes, Nana loved him. And he dreamt of his Mam and Dad in their own home which miraculously turned into a cottage in the country where they were together again, united like in the wedding picture and where it only rained confetti . . .

When Denny awoke next morning, the first thing he saw was the mug of cocoa, stone cold, on the bedside table. The reason he was there flew into his head. This was no stop-over for a night or two. This was the way it was going to be forever.

Bacon-and-egg flavoured air floated up the narrow stairs. Nana never deserted her stove. Home-cooking was her bulwark against the terrors of the world waiting outside 5 Owen Street. Denny went to the minute bathroom, converted from the old boxroom, where he had his own towels mono-grammed 'D' (one of Nana's market bargains) and even his own toothbrush. His reflection in the gilt-rimmed mirror was rumpled, freckled and helpless. The image of a trapped man. Much as he liked Nana, he had the creepy sensation of so much comfort closing in around him like a silken net.

After breakfast, Denny went with Nana to the flat. His Mam was in the main bedroom, sorting piles of her own clothes, choosing items to pack in two big open suitcases. Mam loved pretty dresses but, unlike Nana, she bought them off-the-peg. Denny knew that most of them were from a catalogue, on the never-never, which meant that they weren't paid for yet.

Nana held up a striped blouse. 'Look at this! Blown together! And I bet it cost you a pretty penny, our Trish!'

'Don't start, Mam. You're lucky. You can sew.'

'No luck about it!' Nana flashed back. 'You don't try. Everything has to be instant with you!'

17

Denny had heard this argument many times before. He wandered into the living-room, collecting things he might need at Nana's. Old comics, a roll of sellotape, a plastic car. The room was shabby with scratched, cigarette-burned furniture and stained purple carpeting. The orange blobs on the thin lop-sided curtains clashed horribly.

In Denny's bedroom, Nana was rummaging through his wardrobe and spreading out clothes for inspection. 'You need a good rig-out, my boy! The state of these things!' She was talking loud enough for his mother to hear. Denny felt an early-warning rumble of approaching fuss.

'I'm all right, Nana. I don't want new clothes.'

'Oh, don't you?' Nana glared. She sat down on the edge of the unmade and stale-smelling bed, holding a torn shirt to her chest, her eyes tearful.

'What's the matter, Nana?'

Her voice was sort of cracked. 'I could break my heart,' she said. 'Poor little dab.'

Denny had no idea what she meant. He helped her to pack the garments into a hold-all and a splitting Swift-Save bag. In ten minutes they were on the street, leaving Denny's Mam amid the chaos in the flat.

'What will happen to the furniture, Nana? An' the telly, an' the video—?'

'It's all on the glad-and-sorry. Hire purchase, love. It'll go back where it came from.'

18

Denny was relieved that he'd rescued the sellotape.

'Good morning, Mrs Lewis!' An elderly man came out of a house at the top end of Owen Street. Smartly dressed, he doffed his trilby hat and smiled with two rows of faultless porcelain teeth.

'Cross over!' Nana whipped at Denny. She nodded briefly, dismissing the man who stood gazing at her, his hat in his raised hand. Nana pulled at Denny's arm and walked briskly to the other side of the street.

'Who's that, Nana?'

'Never you mind. Give some people an inch they take a yard.'

Nana often avoided giving a direct answer. Denny wondered if he'd ever understand grown-ups. Nana wasn't old and sour, yet she seemed annoyed because somebody spoke to her.

'Can I go out to see my friends, Nana?'

She unlocked the yellow front door. 'Well—all right. After dinner, though. You can't run about on an empty stomach.'

'I run about on my *feet*, Nana!'

'Oh—a proper comedian, you are! Impudent monkey!' said Nana and they both laughed.

2

'You're going to live at your Nana's then?'

'Yeah. She's not so bad.'

Denny's friend Jayce—proper name Jason Morgan—swung over the high bars, landing awkwardly. 'Ow!'

'Stupid,' said Denny. 'Come on—let's go over the tide.'

'You kiddin'? My Mam'll skin me!' Jayce, fair-haired and grey-eyed, always looked neat and tidy and mostly did what his mother told him.

Denny sighed. 'Better than hangin' around here.'

The play-area hadn't much to offer boys of their age. A few swings, a slide and a climbing frame. That was it. Denny's favourite place was the muddy, grassy shoreline of the Taff mouth, rough tufts of sea-thrift underfoot and the wind gusting a raw, strong smell from the Channel. It was dangerous, yes, the banks falling away steeply into the murk of the mud-bedded river far below or the incoming tide seeping up over the flat ground, sucking at his feet. He'd been warned often enough not to go there but he took no notice. There were official plans to tame the wild tide-fields but before everything concreted into harsh symmetry Denny intended to enjoy the natural untidiness as often as he could. Besides, he had discovered a wonderful fact and was particularly drawn to the river that day.

He kept on niggling at Jayce but it was no use. Jayce was too scared. Denny sighed, defeated. 'What about going over the Centre, then?'

Jayce remembered something. 'Ay—they're forming an under-twelves badminton team. Let's try for it!' Jayce was eager to find a pastime to fill the void of Saturday afternoons. Neither had a talent for football and were half-hearted supporters. It wasn't a whole load of fun standing around perished with cold to watch the Grangers lose every match. Even a visiting girls' side beat them.

'Badminton? Nah . . .' scorned Denny. Then he relented—'Oh—all right, then. Might as well, I s'pose. We can get a Coke there, anyway.'

The Community Centre—red brick, blue pipes and conifer gardens—was a few minutes' walk away. The boys charged up the stairway to the top floor refreshment bar which sold coffee, tea, soft drinks and crinkly packets of junk snacks. A large, aproned lady served behind the hatch. She supplied their order, took their money and called them "My lovelies!' From the double-glazed vista window, the boys had a view of the sweep of Cardiff Bay, the tree-coated headland of Penarth Point jutting out darkly with an old church perched on top.

Denny liked to imagine the olden days, long before he was born, when countless ships steamed or sailed in and out of port, bringing and taking, and Cardiff was the most important place in the world.

'Ay, Den! Did you hear me? The badminton meetin' is downstairs.'

'Yeah . . . well . . . You go on. I might be down later.'

Jayce made a face. 'Bor-ing! Tarra, then.'

The only customer in the bar, Denny took occasional swigs at his canned drink and went on staring at the view, misting over now as cloud formed low over the distant water. Rain spat against the huge expanse of window. The year was struggling to an end. Winter months stretched emptily ahead. And yet, Denny loved the bleak autumn scape of harbour and channel. Unlovely to others' eyes, it held magic for him.

The swing door opened with a swish and a bump.

'Am I late? Where's everybody?' A girl with damp black hair slouched in, her square face moody. Whatsername Price. Gemma. No . . . Emma.

'Late for what?'

Emma threw her canvas bag onto a seat opposite Denny. She sat down and began chewing a large piece of gum.

''Sawright. They said three o'clock. Up here.'

'A meetin', is it?'

'Sort of. See who's interested an' all that.'

A sulky-looking girl, thought Denny. Unsure of herself, he guessed, in spite of her conceited expression.

'Ay—'he began, remembering suddenly, '—if you want to join the badminton, they're downstairs.'

Emma's lips twisted with contempt. 'No fear. I'm here for the dramatics. Thought you were, too.'

Denny perked up. 'Oh! Oh—yeah. I—er—I'll give it a try.'

'They'll give *you* a try. Are you good at actin'? Singin' an' dancin'? I am. My mother's an actress.' She spoke in a slovenly way but she was bossy and a show-off.

Denny stared at her, defiantly. 'Yeah. Sure. I can do all that.'

Emma chewed rapidly and spoke shirtily as she looked away. 'Okay. Don't set your hair on fire. Only talking.'

Denny tried to look unconcerned. She was a horrible sort of girl. She had an outsize chip—more like a log of wood—on her shoulder. His gaze lifted to a bright poster on the wall behind Emma's head.

ALL THOSE INTERESTED IN FORMING A CHILDREN'S STAGE GROUP, PLEASE MEET AT THE CENTRE REFRESHMENT BAR AT 3PM, SATURDAY. AGES 8 to 12. ROB BEVAN WILL LEAD THE MEETING, ASSISTED BY HELEN HARRIS.

Denny was surprised that he hadn't noticed it before. It was big enough. It hit you in the eye—that riot of multi-coloured block lettering.

'Yeah. 'Course. I'd like to do acting,' he said airily. But he was talking to himself. Emma had jumped up to meet two other girls who came rushing in, the three of them breaking into excited chatter. He noticed, though, that the two girls soon left Emma alone and she slouched back to her chair.

The next minute, the room seemed to cram with people. Denny thought that the tall character must be Rob Bevan. Over twenty . . . but not a wrinkly. Decent enough, his longish hair tied back and his clothes respectably worn-out. Keen grey eyes and very white teeth in a tanned face. He looked okay. But Helen Harris—aagh! She was none other than *Miss* Harris who taught a younger class at Denny's school. It was agony enough seeing teachers five days a week without having them around on Saturdays as well. She looked better than usual today though, in white trainers and a blue tracksuit. Not so teacherish.

Denny kept his head down and moved back into the press of damp anoraks and scraping chairs.

'Settle down, everybody!' shouted Rob. There was more scuffling and a few nervous giggles. Rob and Helen Harris each had a clipboard on which they jotted a few headings. 'Give Helen your names, will you? I'll talk while she goes around making the list.'

Helen Harris began with a girl in the front row. Rob raised his voice. 'Right! You're all here because you're interested in forming a drama group . . .'

Not me, thought Denny. I'm here by accident.

'. . . so we'll decide what our first aims will be. We should go for some Music and Movement sessions . . .'

'Ooooo!' went the girls in the back row. Rob held up a hand to quieten them.

'. . . and think about self-discipline,' he continued. 'Acting is a serious business. Acting means teamwork. We'll have fun *but* if you're not prepared to put your mind and energy into the work of the group then pack it in now!'

Denny thought it sounded a bit grim. Rob wouldn't stand for any messing about and he was making that clear at the start. Rob went on talking. He was an actor with a special job, going about starting junior drama groups. He told them about theatres, plays and how acting gave you confidence in public. Denny found himself listening with both ears.

'What's your name?' Helen Harris whispered at Denny's shoulder.

'Oh! Er—Denny Thomas.'

'Dennis, is it?'

'No. Just Denny.'

She wrote his name down neatly and Denny saw that he was numbered 20 on her list. She hadn't yet started the last row so altogether there'd be over thirty in the group if they all joined. Enough to put on something really good. The Sound of Music! Or

Aladdin! Denny had seen both these show at the New Theatre—Nana had taken him—and he had enjoyed them immensely.

Rob was still speaking—'An important decision next! We need a name. What shall we call ourselves?'

Faces went blank and shoulders shrugged up and down.

'Dunno . . .'

'Well—*think*!' yelled Rob, none too pleased. 'Bright sparks, you lot are. This is *your* group. Come on now—! Any ideas?'

Emma Price spoke up. 'The Centre Drama Group?'

Helen Harris, who had finished taking names, printed Emma's suggestion on a large oblong of white paper.

'Any more?'

'Um—what about—um—The Bridge Acting Group?' That was from one of the girls. The first bridge over the Taff heading up river stood solidly in view, girders drenched with rain. Helen Harris wrote down the name.

'Yes—we're near the Clarence Bridge,' said Rob. 'Any more suggestions?'

Denny's hand shot up. 'The Taff Stage Group!'

'I like that,' said Helen Harris, printing it out.

Denny settled back, a little alarmed at hearing his own voice when he had intended to keep his head down and say nothing; but he was pleased with his suggestion. There were no further notions so Helen held up the three possible names and Rob put them to the vote. 'The Taff Stage Group' won by a landslide. Rob said it was a good choice. Even Emma looked happy about it.

'The last thing on the agenda today—our rehearsal room! We can't use the Centre, I'm afraid . . .'

'Aww!' moaned everybody, disappointed. The refreshment bar was a big attraction.

' . . . but we've found a place with a piano in Norton Street. It's a big space upstairs over a lock-up. Should be ideal for us.' Denny's mouth turned down. Norton Street was shut in, part of the grid of terraced houses criss-crossing the suburb. No views of the bay and river from there. Still, he couldn't back out now. He had named the group. This gave him a certain importance. A few of the girls were smiling at him, admiring his cleverness. Denny felt obliged to go on with it, Norton Street or not. And besides, he was interested to know more about drama.

'That's it for today, then,' said Rob. 'We know who we are and where we meet. Next Saturday we'll hold auditions to hear and see what you can do.' The girls giggled and the boys looked awkward. 'Some of you might be natural actors, singers—or have no performing talent at all.'

Emma asked, 'What happens if we're no good on the stage? Do we have to leave the group?'

'Far from it,' Rob said. 'We'll need backstage workers—talented in other ways—to help with scenery, costumes and so on.'

'But don't worry about that now,' added Helen Harris. 'The point of forming the group is to find out what you do best.'

The meeting broke up. Several boys and girls scrambled towards the serving hatch to grab packets of crisps and sweets from the counter. 'Ay—stoppit, you 'ooligans!' shouted the lady behind the counter. Somehow she managed to sort out who owed what for what.

'Okay, then! Two o'clock next Saturday at Norton Street. Thanks, everybody!' Rob yelled over the din of the now unruly crowd. He gave Helen Harris a wry smile. They had lost control for that day.

In the confusion, Jayce came bounding through the swing doors.

'Ay—why didn't you come to the meeting?' he demanded, giving Denny a friendly push.

'Went to another meeting, didn' I?'

'What meeting?' Jayce frowned, wondering what he'd missed. As they left the Centre, Denny told him all about it. At first Jayce hooted with laughter. 'You're goin' on the *stage*?'

'Well—not right away. We'll sort of work up to it, I expect. Learn things. Training, like.'

Jayce sniffed. 'Sounds a bit like school!'

But Denny could tell that Jayce was curious because he asked lots more questions and, sure enough, Jayce wanted to know—'Is it too late to join?'

'Shouldn't think so.' Denny mentioned the next meeting at Norton Street. 'But what about you playing badminton?'

'Nah! I'm not doin' that. You got to have proper gear and rackets. My Mam won't fork out any more. Not since I lost my bike.'

'Oh. Oh, well. Come to Norton Street, then.'

'Yeah. Might be good for a laugh.'

Jayce, though, wasn't laughing. He was almost swaggering. Denny marvelled that so many people thought that they'd be good at acting and Jayce was clearly one of them. Well, they'd see . . .

Outside the Centre gates, Denny turned to the right going towards the river.

'I gotta go home,' objected Jayce, refusing to follow.

'Aw—come on, Jayce! Don't be a spoilsport! Only for a walk. The rain's stopped now.'

Jayce was reluctant and grumbled as he straggled after Denny until they came to the river edge. The tide was out and the exposed mud lay in thick folds in shades from grey to black.

'See?' Denny was pointing to a pool down river. 'That's it!'

'Can't see nothin'!'

'The Magic Pool! It must be. It's not like the rest of the river. It never dries up. It goes down an' down. Bottomless.'

'Gerraway!' Jayce scorned.

'It's true! There's always water there—even in the summer when the tide's low and the mud's all cracked like—like a jig-saw puzzle.' In summer droughts Denny had noticed wading-birds coming in to drink at the reliable watering-place. And he had found out something interesting about it. More than that. Exciting. They walked on, hunching into their anoraks against the wind.

'Yeah. Well. Just 'cos there's water there don't mean it's *magic*.' Jayce didn't have much imagination.

'It's a legend. Some of those old stories are true, Jayce. I found out about the pool in a book.'

'Oh, *books*! I'm goin' home for my tea. It's freezin' out here.'

'Hang on a sec! See that swirly bit in the middle? Well, it sucks people down an' they're never seen again!'

'What people? Nobody with any sense'd go out there.'

'Well, if they did they'd be sucked down. Or a small boat could be swallowed up if it went over that spot when the river's high.'

Jayce was not convinced. 'I never heard of anybody vanishin'. Are you sure?'

'Yeah! An' there's more. A sea monster lives down there an' he can change into a green lady an' she waves an' calls to people so that they go to her—not knowin' that she's really a monster that'll eat them up.'

'Loada rubbish,' said Jayce.

Danny wasn't dismayed by Jayce's lack of interest in the magic pool. He turned away, eager to slither down the bank, risking soiling his clothes. Suddenly, from the corner of his eye he saw a movement downstream. A ramshackle hut, barely holding together, sheltered in the crook of the river bend. Someone or something had briefly appeared and then quickly taken cover behind the rotting boards.

'Did you see that, Jayce?'

Jayce stood close to Denny. Denny whispered— 'There's somebody in the old hut . . .'

'Might be a tramp. One of them homeless layabouts. Mam says I musn't go near anybody like that. Anyway, I didn't see anybody. Come *on*. Denny.'

'Not their fault, is it? If they haven't got a home?' Denny thought that he might be a bit homeless himself if it wasn't for Nana.

Jayce didn't answer but just shrugged and walked away. This time, Denny followed Jayce as they crossed the rough ground leading back to the streets. The story about the magic pool sounded far-fetched, Denny supposed, and perhaps he was carried away in the telling of it. But why shouldn't it be true? Wales had heaps of mysteries. Wales was well-known for legends about princes and wizards and dragons and monsters . . . Because he and his friends lived in a shabby, unromantic part of Wales, it didn't mean that they should be left out of the magic. The river had an irresistible appeal for him. He wanted—needed—to believe in the whirlpool and the monster and the green lady.

As they parted to go to their different streets, Denny felt sorry for Jayce. Life would be very dull without a few bottomless pools and a monster or two.

'See you, then,' said Jayce.

'Yeah. See you.'

'In Norton Street?' said Nana in surprise. 'That must be the old Planet!'

'It's up a stairway over a lock-up place.'

'That's right, love.' Nana's eyes shone. 'The Planet Dance Hall, it was. Oh—donkey's years ago. When I was young, I lost my engagement ring there. Never found it.'

The term 'dance hall' confused Denny. He didn't exactly know what it was. 'You mean you went there to discos?'

Nana explained—'Dances, not discos. Well, our

dances were like discos in one way. The music was from records—old 78s—on a wind-up gramophone. Yes! Seems funny now—but it was the same idea as a disco. No big sound systems, though. Not then. We could hear ourselves speak in those days. A lot of courting there was on the dance floor.'

'Courting?'

'Well, we called it that. Chatting-up, that sort of thing.'

Denny could see that Nana liked remembering.

'The bigger dance halls, up town, had proper live bands to play for them. The musicians used to wear posh evening clothes—you know, black suits and bow ties. Girls used to get crushes on them, like they do with pop stars now.'

Nana had spent a lot of her youth dancing, from what she said, and that accounted for her being so good at it. 'Wednesday, Friday and Saturday evening, the dances were held. Threepence to go in! Old pence, I mean. Oh dear! the good times we had at The Planet!'

Denny was intrigued but also hungry. He began setting the table for tea while Nana talked from the stove. She waved the fish slice. 'I'd run up a pretty dress on my Mam's sewing machine and off I'd go to enjoy myself. Sometimes, you'd think the floor would give way, it got so hectic!'

'Did you always go to the Planet, Nana?'

'Nearly always. It was near home. No waiting about for buses and no fares to pay. And we didn't dislike dancing to records. It was better music than you got from some of the live bands. Some of them were hopeless—couldn't keep good time.'

Nan attended to the sizzling frying pan and its hopping beads of fat. 'Well, well!' she sighed, 'You'll be going to the dear old Planet!' Then she asked— 'What for, love?'

Denny had told her but patiently he explained again.

'Oh, yes . . . Acting and singing! I wanted to go on to the stage,' Nana sighed, 'But my father was too strict. He said no—so I went to work in the cigar factory instead.' Nan's eyes were wistful, remembering her disappointment.

'Rob Bevan says the place in Norton Street will be good for rehearsals and training classes.'

Nan dished up the triangular pieces of fish.

'There was a good sprung floor at the Planet,' she said. 'Lovely for dancing. I hope it hasn't got woodworm.'

After their fish tea, Denny and Nana sorted through his clothes. Despite Denny's protests, Nana put some of them in the backyard bin.

'You look like something out of the rag-bag!' she tutted.

Denny gave almost no thought to his appearance.

True, he'd have liked a new pair of trainers but otherwise he was quite satisfied.

In the back-kitchen, Nana stuffed Denny's remaining washable clothes into her top loader.

'The water's hot. Have a nice bath, Denny. Off you go, love. Wash your hair and be sure to scrub your nails.'

Denny sighed. If Nana had a fault, it was her mania for making him have frequent hot baths. 'She'd *boil* me if she could,' he muttered, stumping upstairs. His parents often forgot to check up on his bathing, which gave him more freedom. You could waste a lot of your life, messing about in bathrooms. It was fun, though, steaming up the walls and mirror and writing his name in the condensation; and he had to admit that he felt better after washing away the grime of days.

Squeaky-clean though he was, Nana was still on the warpath. 'Early to bed, early to rise!' she said.

'Aw, Nana! Let me see the cowboy film on telly!'

'Well . . . all right, then. Just the one film, mind. We're going up the market first thing tomorrow morning. I want to see you up with the lark—bright and fresh.'

In the warm kitchen, Denny settled into the armchair to watch the film. Horses galloped and guns fired on a Western ranch where the cowboys' hats never fell off, no matter how hard they rode and fought. Perhaps their Stetsons are stuck on with

35

glue, Denny thought. After all, they're *acting*. Not real cowboys . . . He wondered if he'd ever be a film star. The Taff Stage Group might be the start of great things.

3

The Sunday morning market attracted a mixed crowd. Some were eager to buy bargains from the cheap goods on display and others were content to stroll around, 'just looking' and generally enjoying the atmosphere. The biting rain had gone overnight. The dazzling autumn day, a late gift, brought back a hint of summer. Stalls flapped with clothes suspended on lines, china was piled in precarious heaps and hamburger stalls did a roaring trade.

A young man, knee-deep in chunky parcels of polyester, hollered—'Only three pound for a pair of these best quality double sheets! Come on, girls!' A few women laughed and dipped into their bags for money. They liked the prices and the good-humoured entertainment.

Denny trailed after Nana through the crush, listening to snatches of conversations. 'Have you noticed—'a man said to his companion—'that Aunty Blod has stopped wearing those old browns and blues. She's all red and green now!' 'I'll wallop you, our Tristan!' an angry mother bellowed at her obstreperous son. He looked about six and nasty with it. 'Did you knock over those elephants?' A tarted-up girl said with disdain to her friend—'I'm not buyin' nuthin' *yet*! I bet it all fell off a lorry!' Music poured from transistors and a thousand voices from Cardiff and beyond added to the noise.

'Come on, Denny!' Nana tugged his sleeve, pulling him into a covered stall where rows of racks were crammed with casual clothes for kids. Nana began lifting hangers from the racks, examining shirts, jackets and jeans. Denny flinched, hoping that he would not meet anybody he knew. Any second, he would be forced to try on various garments.

'Pop on this anorak, Den!' said Nana, her arms filled with a selection from the racks. To Denny's relief, the stall-holder, a man with a gentle dark olive face, took them to a quiet spot at the back of the display. There, Denny didn't mind so much while Nana fussed and fretted, buttoning, zipping and tying him into a succession of new clothes. At last she let him go and he was comfortable in his old ones again.

Nana paid the man, then she and Denny wandered out into the crush of the crowd, each carrying two bulging striped carrier-bags. They passed a stall festooned with dress materials.

'Hello, Albert!' Nana called to a fat man. Albert was measuring out a long piece of woollen suiting.

'Hello, there! Some nice winter fabrics in today, Mrs Lewis! Take a look, my love!'

'Next week!' promised Nana. 'This is my grandson. We've been kitting him out!'

Denny was glad that Nana wasn't stopping to buy but he felt slightly guilty, too. He guessed that she couldn't afford anything for herself, not after spending a small fortune on him.

'One more stall, Den, and then we'll go home. Over here, love.'

At a long table set out with hundreds of pairs of shoes and boots, Nana found trainers to suit Denny. He couldn't stop his grin of delight when he put them on. 'Great! Thanks, Nana!' Then, as he looked up from admiring his smart footwear, Denny's neck tingled. He glanced over his shoulder. Just like the day before, he had a keen sensation that somebody was watching him.

'What's the matter, Den?'

'Uh? Oh—nothin', Nana.'

'Do they fit properly? They don't pinch? Can you waggle your toes?'

'Mm? Oh—the trainers. Yeah—they're great, Nana!'

'Keep them on, then.' While Nana shoved the old trainers into another plastic bag and paid a lady for the new ones, Denny had another chance to look back. Once again, he thought that somebody dodged out of sight, like at the old hut on the riverside. Silly.

There were hundreds of people going in and out of the stalls. Why should anybody want to hide from *him?* Loada rubbish, as Jayce would say.

'Come on, love. My legs have had enough for one day,' said Nana. So they carried their bags through the jostle of people and made their way home. Denny's trainers startled the eyes, white as new snow in sunshine. Secretly, he tried to scuff them up a bit. They were brilliant. In a couple of days, when they were worn in more to his liking, they'd be even more brilliant. Denny was quietly happy. He forgot, for the time being, the creepy feeling of being watched . . .

Ben Sarami sat next to Denny in class at Junior School. Ben's family kept a mini-market—selling everything from cooking oil to daily newspapers—around the corner from Owen Street. Nana shopped there for groceries and sent Denny there on messages to fetch the odd item she'd forgotten or had run out of. Ben helped his parents in the shop after school and at weekends. He had learnt early to handle money and was quick at arithmetic, never making mistakes.

'Ben—you can work out this sum, can't you?'

'Yes, Mrs Howells.' Ben dealt with the figures confidently, his large dark eyes clear and intelligent.

'Well done.' Mrs Howells, thin and neat, ticked Ben's correct answer. 'Now show Denny how to do it.'

Arithmetic was not Denny's strong point. 'Don't be scared,' said Ben. 'It's easy.'

Mrs Howells had thirty pupils to teach and she sometimes asked them to help one another. Denny relaxed. He understood when Ben explained how to solve the problems.

'Girls' computer time now!' Mrs Howells called out. The boys had been guilty of grabbing the computer and using it twice as much as the girls, so they were allotted equal time each week. Louise Parry was a whizz at computers—best in the class. Often, girls and boys paired for computer time and then Denny tried to work with Louise before anybody else snapped her up.

'Don't panic. You have a different kind of brain,' Louise would tell him when he was confused. 'Look how clever you are, makin' up poetry an' readin' aloud to the class.'

Denny had made up his mind to work hard at maths and computer skills so that he wasn't completely nowhere in those subjects. Words, though, came easily to him. Louise was right about that. He had read most of the books in the school library and was always on the look-out for more. Mrs Howells often suggested books he should read and, with her help, he had joined the big Lending Library where there was a well-stocked children's section. It was there that Denny had found the book of Welsh legends and read about the Magic Pool of the River Taff.

'Look what you're doing, Denny. Seven and nine make sixteen,' Ben pointed out.

'Sorry. Stupid mistake. I wasn't concentrating. Can you come out on Saturday afternoon, Ben?'

Ben's face went solemn. 'I don't know. The shop is busy then.'

At this point, Mrs Howells looked at their work so Denny put off talking to Ben until after school.

Later, in the scramble through the main door, a voice called out 'Don't run! Watch the traffic!' Miss Helen Harris came towards Denny and his friends. 'Hello, Denny. You won't forget the Stage Group on Saturday?'

'I won't forget, Hel—er—Miss. Um—Jayce, here, wants to join. And Ben might—when I've told him what it's about.'

Ben look mystified.

'The more the merrier,' said Helen Harris. 'See you on Saturday!' She left them and walked to her car.

Denny went out through the school gate with Ben. 'There's this new thing, see, called the Taff Stage Group. Ask your Dad if you can join, Ben.'

Ben shook his head.

'I don't think he will consent. My father needs me. I am learning the retail trade.' At times, Ben seemed to be almost grown-up. 'But I will ask him.'

41

A girl pushed past them at a run, almost knocking Jayce to the ground. 'Ay! Mind out!' Jayce had a quick temper and he sent the girl spinning around. She stood there, glowering at them.

'Oh—er—hi!' said Denny. It was Emma Price. 'Emma's in the Taff Stage Group,' he told the others.

'Har! Har! Think you can act?' taunted Jayce. 'That'll be a scream, seein' *you* thuddin' about!'

Emma scowled at Jayce, annoyed at the reference to her clumsiness. 'Why don't you mind your own business? My mother's an actress. I'll be better at it than a *worm* like you!' She gave Jayce a hefty push so that he fell back against Denny and Ben.

'That will do!' commanded a deep voice. 'Don't you know it's dangerous to push and shove on the pavement? When are you going to learn some sense?'

'Look out! It's Pop Lollipop!'

The elderly man, swathed in a shabby overcoat and woolly scarves, held his crossing sign aloft with the authority of Neptune and his trident. It was rumoured that he was a sailor in the Big War and had been torpedoed more times that they'd had hot dinners. He certainly wasn't afraid of a gang of scruffy kids.

'Stand quiet, 'til I give the order to cross! No fooling about on deck!'

Meekly, they waited. Plans, stories and words were shaping in Denny's mind.

'Is this it?' Denny, Jayce, Emma Price and some others stood before a closed wooden door set flat in the brick wall at the far end of Norton Street. About twenty children had turned up.

A man put his head out of an upper window of a house across the street. ''Ang on! Just a sec! I'll be there in a minute!' With this muddled promise the man withdrew and slammed down the sash-window.

Rob Bevan and Helen Harris drove up in Helen's car as the man hobbled out of his house, pulling on a crumpled cardigan, slippers slopping on his feet. His crumpled red face was topped with wisps of gingery hair which had seen better days.

'Hello, Mr Hopkins,' Rob said. 'We're early, I think.'

'You said two o'clock. It's only quarter-to,' Mr Hopkins grumbled. He jangled a collection of keys and fitted one into the lock of the wooden door. He led them up a flight of creaky stairs covered with dirt-encrusted, cracked lino. At the top, Mr Hopkins unlocked another door which swung inwards.

''Ere you are,' said Mr Hopkins. 'I've 'ad the radiator on all morning.'

The room was long and dark, with two dingy windows set on either side. The floor was made up of narrow boards, broken and splintered in places and blackened with the trodden-in grime of years. In one corner a pile of wooden chairs, mostly broken, and a stack of card-tables were pushed together haphazardly. Bulky objects lay beneath the cover of a tattered bedspread. The air was acrid with old dust and a faint, painty smell came from the single old-fashioned radiator.

Denny gulped. Was this Nana's Planet? The place where she had twirled about in her pretty frocks, dancing to record music and enjoying the compliments of her young partners? He had imagined it in bright colours, new and clean. But, of course, Nana's threepenny dances were held a long time ago . . .

Mr Hopkins snapped on the light—an unshaded bulb dangling from the ceiling. ''Ere's the old Joanna!' He showed Rob and Helen the battered upright piano standing against the wall. 'You might get a tune out of it.'

Rob, Helen, Denny and the others stood around, silently surveying the home of the Taff Stage Group.

'Well—I'll leave you to get on with it. Be out by four o'clock. I'll be over to lock up then. I likes to get that done before the Football Results on the telly.' Mr Hopkins slip-slopped away through the door and down the grimy stairs. When they heard the street door slam shut, they all shouted with laughter.

'Not exactly what we expected!' gasped Rob Bevan. 'Ha! ha! Try the piano, Helen!'

Helen fingered the octaves. An off-key, discordant twanging came up from the depths of the frame. Boinng! Bee-oinng! This set everybody off laughing again. Helen turned and shrugged her shoulders, her face pained.

'Oh, have mercy!' laughed Rob. 'My fault! I should have inspected the place before I booked it. Still, it's cheap and warm. We'll be all right.'

Rob and a few of the children set up chairs and they all settled down.

Emma was looking around, particularly at the dirt-coated window panes. 'We could clean it up,' she suggested. The boys groaned. 'Yeah—an' you lot will have to pitch in an' help.'

'Okay—we'll make it more presentable. But not today. We're here to hold auditions.' Rob gave out some pieces of paper with typing on them.

Denny had a tight feeling in his throat. Emma looked nervous and Jayce was staring at the door as if he might make a run for it. Stage fright, thought Denny. We've all got stage fright.

'Two minutes for study and then we'll hear you,' Rob said. Heads went down and they began going over their lines.

When the time was up, Emma was asked to read first. She stood in a lumpish way in front of the others and began to read. As she brought out the words, her jaws moved in a chewing motion. Helen held up a hand for Emma to stop.

'Are you eating something, Emma?'

'Yeah. A toffee.'

Rob sighed. 'Sit down, Emma. When you've finished eating, you can read. Now get this, all of you. You are not spending two hours of rehearsal time every Saturday, stuffing your faces with sweets and snacks. Leave it out! Right?'

Everybody nodded. They looked a bit ashamed of Emma. By the time she was twenty she'd have no teeth left. Denny was told to read next. He began with a squeak and he heard Jayce snort. Rob took it calmly.

'Lower your voice a little. Start again.'

This time, Denny read without a single fault.

There was a silence. Then everybody clapped and one or two of the boys whistled. Denny's face went hot.

'Good, Denny. Very good,' said Rob quietly.

At the end of the readings, while Rob and Helen compared notes, the others spoke enthusiastically to Denny. 'You were fantastic!' 'You'll get the star part!'

'Emma was good, too,' said Denny and everybody agreed. To their surprise, Emma read well when she stood up with her shoulders back and spoke in a clear, toffeeless voice.

'Oh, well . . .' Emma said. Oddly, she had gone back to her ordinary, ungainly self. Perhaps she needed an audience to bring out the best in her, Denny thought.

Jayce alone had read hesitantly, putting no meaning into his words. 'I'm useless,' he said.

Denny began to say 'Don't put yourself down, Jayce . . .'

'Hello! I am here.' They looked around to see Ben standing in the doorway. 'I have permission to join your group.'

'That's great! Come in, Ben!'

Ben half-turned. 'I have brought Louise with me. She was lost. She wishes to join, too.'

Louise stepped into the room behind Ben. Her round brown face beamed at the crowd. 'What a funny place!' she said.

'We thought it was a dump at first—but it's fine,' said Emma.

Denny took Ben and Louise over to meet Rob and Helen. They were shy for a minute or two but when the room quietened down again they both read capably.

Rob looked happy. 'We have plenty of good speaking voices. Next week we'll bring taped music and have a try at movement. Now, then. What are we going to do for our first production?'

Denny's thoughts raced for a moment. Should he mention his idea? Why not? Well . . . everybody might think it was stupid . . . No, they wouldn't. He'd thought up the group name, hadn't he? He took a deep breath. Then he began to tell the story of the Taff Magic Pool and the Green Lady who changed into the Monster. 'We—er—could do a sort of play about it . . . perhaps . . .' he trailed off, not knowing what more to say.

At once, Helen Harris said she thought it was a marvellous idea with masses of potential. She talked like that. Rob agreed. Denny felt awkward at being the centre of attention again.

Rob said—'How about that, then? Shall we devise a drama about the Magic Pool of the River Taff?'

'Yeah! Wow!' 'Ooooh!'

Helen Harris said she would read everything she could about the legend before the next meeting and make a rough outline for the play.

Rob looked at his watch. 'Nearly four o'clock . . .'

'Awww!'

'Yes—well—Mr Hopkins wants to lock up—'

'—before the Football Results!' everybody shouted in chorus.

'Look nippy, then! Tidy the chairs away. Same time, same place next week!'

Denny and Ben did their best to cheer up Jayce on the way home.

'You can act a part without speaking,' said Denny.

'Mm. I hope so. I can't talk with everybody lookin' at me. Not as easy as you'd think. Anyway, I'd never be able to learn the words off by heart.'

Jayce was depressed but they ended up joking before they reached home. 'P'raps I can move the scenery! Tarra! See you!' Jayce went towards his street and Denny went on with Ben.

'I'm glad you joined the stage group, Ben. Good fun!'

'It is. Next time, I shall be early. Today, I helped with filling the shelves in the shop but next week I do not have to do that.'

'See you Ben!' Denny ran off down Owen Street. He could hardly wait to tell Nana about the meeting in the old Planet Dance Hall. As he neared the house, he saw Nana standing on the doorstep—a thing he had never seen before—a jacket caped over her shoulders. Anxious lines pulled her mouth down. Something was wrong.

'Nana?'

'Go in, love. Your tea's on the table. I might be a minute or two out here. Don't look so worried. I'm all right.'

Denny went past her into the kitchen. On the table was a plate of congealing chips and a mini pork pie. A packet of biscuits lay unopened beside the unappetising meal. He closed the kitchen door to keep out the draught from the passage. What was the matter with Nana? He bit into the pastry. Not Nana's idea of a good tea—nor his. What had happened? The afternoon's enjoyment disappeared into a tight band around his forehead. He didn't understand this upset to the cosy sameness of Nana's home. It was his haven. His rock. One world of his had fallen apart

49

and now ... It—it wasn't *right*. He munched gloomily, hoping that Nana would soon be her normal self again. It was as if a cold blast had taken the smile off her face and chilled her to the bone. At last, he heard voices and then Nana came into the kitchen, removing her coat.

'Here I am, love! Sorry about the scrappy tea. I—er—had a bit of bad news. A—a friend of mine is ill. Nothing for you to worry about.'

Denny looked at her straight. 'What friend?'

'Oh—you wouldn't know who it is. Look—let me cook you something nice ...'

'No. This'll do, Nana. It's fine, thank you.'

For the first time in his life, Denny didn't believe a word that Nana said. She was telling him *lies*. Not nasty lies—but not the truth. Keeping something from him. Nana gave him a smile and looked more at ease.

'When you're at school on Monday I'm going to visit my—friend. She's in hospital. But she's going to be all right.'

Oh. That seemed fair enough. Wouldn't he be worried if Jayce was in hospital? Or Ben? Or Emma or Louise?

'Okay, Nana.' Now he knew why she'd been standing on the street. Mrs Morris, opposite, had a telephone and she made calls and took urgent messages for the neighbours. Nana had been waiting for a call about her friend, to find out about visiting the hospital.

'How was your acting group, Den?' Nana never forgot to ask about his day, no matter how tired or busy she was.

'It was good, Nana. I like the Planet. It's gone a bit old and dusty but we're going to tidy it up. Mr Hopkins is all right. I think he owns it.'

'Oh—dear old Oppo!' she smiled. 'Yes—he owns it. When I was a girl it belonged to his father. Oppo was a lovely dancer!'

Anything less likely, Denny couldn't imagine. 'Well, he does the football pools now. I expect he's given up dancing,' Denny said. Denny wondered if Mr Hopkins was one of the boys who had chatted up Nana—and if that man with the trilby had been another. Grown-ups were a big mystery. They had a secret life of their own, made up of memories and old letters and photographs—and whispers when they didn't want you to know too much.

'I thought I'd go over the Centre tomorrow, Nana,' Denny said innocently.

Nana was staring into the fire, probably thinking about her friend in the hospital. 'Mm? Yes, that's all right, love.'

Denny had arranged with Jayce to go to the Centre first and then go over the tide-field to have a good look at the Magic Pool. Miss Helen Harris called this 'research'. Later, the whole group might go to see it, to get the feeling right for their play.

Suddenly, though, thoughts of the Magic Pool were pushed aside and Denny pictured the tumbledown hut on the river-bank. Who had been hiding there? Was it the same person who had dodged out of sight at the market? Jayce would say that Denny had an overheated imagination but in Denny's mind was the firm belief that the shadowy person existed and, for some reason, that person was watching him.

4

The incoming tide brought a squall, blowing and rattling anything that moved outside the Community Centre. Denny and Jayce could hardly walk into the pushing wind and the rain which slanted against them in torrents as they made their way along the river bank.

'Ugh! Let's go home, Denny! There's nothin' to see!'

'There might be! Come *on*, Jayce. Don't be such a wet blanket!'

'A wha—?'

'A wet blanket! A person who can't see the fun in anythin'?'

'Fun! This is *torture*. Wet blanket! A soakin' wet Jason, you mean!'

Denny's anger surged up. 'All right, then—don't bother! I'm sick of hearin' you grumblin'!' He was forced to shout, competing with the howling, cracking wind which swooped down, snatching away the sound of his voice.

'Suits me!' Jayce yelled back. 'I'm goin'! You'll fall in the tide one day! The Monster will get you! Har! har!' Laughing and jeering, Jayce ran off over the fields, back to the wind-break of the houses.

Denny turned his back on the power of the gale so that it whistled past the hood of his anorak. His eyes smarted, running with moisture which he wiped away with the back of his hand. The storm was rough enough to take his breath away but he and Jayce had braved worse weather . . . Some friend! The wind eased and Denny turned, stumbling onward. Oh, well. He was partly to blame. He'd gone over the top shouting at Jayce who probably was bored with so much talk about the Magic Pool. Jayce might have gone off the idea of the Magic Pool drama, too, because he hadn't read well at the auditions.

Swirls of water were now rushing in from the Channel. The heavy rain had softened the edge of the steep bank where Denny walked so that every step was a slither and slide to the next one, mud splurging up to the ankles of his new trainers . . .

The Magic Pool! There! A piece of driftwood whirled helplessly, circling in and in, then spiralling rapidly until it was pulled under by the strong current at the pool centre. Denny began to run, hoping to find more wood to throw into the pool. He crossed the narrow but deep gulley which cut into the field, leaping it triumphantly.

'Go back . . .!' Did he hear a voice? Or was it the cry of the distressed gulls, winging inland? Difficult to tell in the raging and battering wind. The old hut was only yards away . . . Denny stopped, sensing another presence, seeing another shadow. Then he turned away from the river and, slipping and lurching, ran as fast as he could for the safety of the streets.

'*Dennny*! Oh, Denny . . . Look at you!'

Denny stood in Nana's back kitchen, mud to the knees of his jeans.

'You've been over the tide!'

'Yes, Nana. Sorry, Nana.'

'Come here to me. Take off those wet things. Oh dear! No wonder your Mam gives up on your clothes! And I thought I could trust you to be sensible!'

'I'm all right, Nana. A bit of mud won't hurt me.'

Nana stooped and unlaced the sopping, mud-coated trainers, their white newness gone forever.

'Get your jeans off. And your jumper and

54

underthings.' She gave him clean, warm clothes from the airing rack and she rubbed hard at his hair with a rough towel. Nana was angry and saddened. Her silence said more than words. Denny felt shame at his stupidity and lack of care. She had spent her money on new clothes for him and he had ruined them.

She put the towel aside and held him by the arms so that he had to look at her. 'Now listen to me, my boy. The river fascinates you. I know that. But it's dangerous! It can change in a second—and sweep you away. Denny—children have been drowned in the Taff!'

Denny nodded. Nana went on—'You've been warned all your life. You know about that treacherous old tide. *So why do you go there?*'

'Sorry, Nana. But—it's—it's the Magic Pool! I found it!'

Nana looked puzzled. She said, 'Let's sit in front of the fire and you can tell me about it. At the moment you're talking double-Dutch.'

Denny told Nana the whole story. Well . . . not quite the whole story. He still said nothing about the secret watcher. That was nothing to do with the Magic Pool and, besides, he had no proof. Only a creepy feeling . . .

'A legend!' Nana said when Denny had finished talking. 'It's a good idea to use it for your stage group. I can imagine it!'

'Can you, Nana?' She was great like that. She never told him to shut up or said he was talking nonsense. She listened. And, like him, she could think herself into the scene . . .

'Oh, yes . . . I can see it. The Green Lady!—sort of silvery green seaweed dripping down from her arms—and the Monster all grey and scaly . . .'

'Yeah! I can see them, too, Nana . . .!'

Nana remembered her responsibilities and she pulled up sharp. 'Yes—well—it's a good story, Den. I like it very much. Nobody enjoys a good tale more than I do. But a story is a story. Keep it in its place. Now then. Back to basics. No more playing about near the river! Understand? Promise me you won't go there!'

Denny had no choice in the matter. 'I promise, Nana. I'm sorry I worried you—an' I'm sorry about my clothes.'

Nana was already on her way to the washing-machine. 'I'll deal with this lot, don't worry. You can clean up your trainers when they're dry.'

Later, as he scraped at the caked mud, Denny asked—'Do I still get a birthday present from you, Nana?'

Nana was ironing his freshly washed and dried shirt. 'You don't deserve one!' Then her face softened into a smile. 'But—yes—you can have your skates.'

Denny coughed. 'Herm—! I—er—I don't want skates now, Nana.'

'Oh? What, then?'

'I—um—I think I'd like binoculars,' Denny said casually. Then he ended in a rush—'I'll be able to see the Magic Pool from the big window upstairs at the Community Centre. I needn't go anywhere near the tide! Not if I have . . . *binoculars*!'

It was a marvellous brainwave. Nana looked at him, half laughing, as if he was a hopeless case.

'Trust you to think of a way round it! Oh dear! You're a character, you are! All right, love. Binoculars.'

Denny scraped happily. His trainers were looking good. A well-worn dirty white. Nobody would ever guess that he'd only worn them twice.

On the second Saturday at Norton Street, Rob played taped music and Helen gave out copies of her notes on the Magic Pool legend.

'I didn't find out much more,' Helen told them. 'How about you, Denny?'

'Well—I went to the place where I think the pool is. It's sort of dark and swirly.' He didn't mention his promise to Nana. He didn't want to sound like a baby who couldn't take care of himself.

Denny took a folded exercise book from his pocket. 'I wrote a—um—a story about the Monster and the Magic Pool. I—er—made it up out of my head.'

'Great. Read it, Denny,' Rob said.

So Denny began. 'One evening in olden times, the River Taff was peaceful in the mist. Very calm and still. On the river bank, a young prince waited, wondering how he could cross to the other side. He wore a golden crown and a golden belt over his tunic. He had no boat and there was no bridge. Suddenly, in mid-river, he saw a shape shining with a pale green light. Slowly, the shape changed until the prince saw that it was a lady. A Green Lady. She was very beautiful. Her gown was green, her hair was green and trails of silvery-black-green seaweed fell from her outstretched arms. "Prince! Prince! I will help you to cross the river," she called.'

Denny paused. Nobody spoke so he went on—'The prince said—"Thank you, lovely Green Lady. You are most kind." Thinking that there might be a stone bridge beneath the water, the prince waded out to meet the Green Lady.

' "Walk towards me!" she called. Her voice echoed over the still, deep water. "Take my hand!" The prince was so far out in the river that he was glad of the Green Lady's offer to guide him. He touched the tips of her fingers. They were wet and cold, cold, cold . . . "One more step, Prince!" said the lady. As he moved forward, the river changed. Where the Green Lady stood, the water began to churn around and around. The noise was terrible as the water swirled and thundered past the prince, catching him in its crazy circle. "Ha! ha! hee!" screamed the Green Lady and then—*she* changed! The green light faded and, in place of the beautiful lady, a huge sea-grey Monster with a coat of iron scales heaved up from the middle of the pool, rolling purple eyes and baring long jagged teeth at the prince. "Aagh!" the prince cried out. "I have been tricked!" "Urgh! urgh!" roared the Monster. "You are in the Magic Pool! It goes down and down without end. You cannot escape!" "Aargh!" shouted the prince as the Monster grabbed him and drew him into the eddying water of the Magic Pool.'

Denny stopped. Again, nobody spoke or moved. Mouths had dropped open and eyes were round and staring.

'Oo-er,' said Emma. 'Go on, Den.'

Denny looked at Rob and Helen and they nodded. Denny took up the story. 'The river became still again. There was no sign of the Monster, the Green Lady or the poor unlucky prince.

'Now, in that place, nobody ever spoke of the Magic Pool and the evil Monster for they were too afraid and fishermen in their small boats took care to keep away from that part of the river. A few weeks later, on a calm, misty evening, another prince arrived at the river bank. He wore a golden tunic, a golden belt and a golden crown studded with sparkling jewels worth millions of pounds. But his riches were of no use to him because he had no boat in which to cross the river. No matter how many jewels he offered them, all the fishermen shook their heads and rowed swiftly away. The prince sat down on the river bank. He was tired and hungry. His only food was a crust of bread which he carried in a bag tied to his golden belt. He decided to keep the crust until he was really starving. How stupid he was! He should have asked the fishermen to sell him some fish but they had all gone away. In despair, the prince looked around. He narrowed his eyes. Down river, he saw a disgraceful old hut, the roof half fallen in and the walls rotting. He walked towards it, hoping that somebody lived there. Somebody who would be able to help him.'

Denny wondered if everybody was getting bored by this time so he looked up and asked 'D'you want me to go on?'

'Yeah!' said Jayce. 'Don't stop now. We want to know how it ends!'

So Denny began again. 'The prince drew close to the old hut and he looked inside. It was empty except for a pile of dirty rags jumbled up in a dark corner. "Do you wish to speak with me?" A shaky old voice came from the rags and a little wrinkled man peeped out. The prince had never seen such an ancient person before, so thin that his bones stuck out like sticks. The prince was kind at heart. He

60

forgot his own troubles. "Poor old man! When did you last eat any food?" "Oh . . . ages ago, bach. About twenty years, I think." "That's terrible!" said the prince angrily, thinking of the laden banquets far away in his castle. "I am known as the Old Hermit. Nobody ever comes near me," quivered the old man. The prince opened his bag. "Look here—" he said, "— have this crust of bread. Eat, Old Hermit. You are very welcome to it." The old man chewed the bread with his gummy mouth, smiling happily. "I wish I had more food to give you," the prince said. "When I cross the river I shall buy lots of tasty morsels and bring them back for you." But as the prince was speaking, something strange was happening to the Old Hermit. The crinkly little face became smooth and round. The stick arms and stick legs grew steady and firm. Glossy white hair flowed to the Old Hermit's shoulders and his eyes were bright and keen. The prince fell back, amazed. The Old Hermit was still old but now he was sturdy and fit and well, in the best of health! His voice did not tremble but it rang out deep and strong. "One act of kindness had the power to give me my strength, O Prince!" The prince could not speak. "The Green Lady of The Magic Pool put a spell on me, many years ago. Until your crust of bread restored me to the pink of condition, I was doomed to crawl about, a weak old crumbly bag of bones!" "This is wonderful!" said the prince. "But what Magic Pool? And who is the Green Lady? She sounds very nasty." They sat on the river bank together and the Old Hermit told the prince about the horrible danger waiting for anybody tempted by the Green Lady to cross the river. He pointed to a large stone. "Only you can move that boulder. Do it at once." The prince obeyed and moved the stone easily. Beneath it was a ring with a bright green jewel in it. "Take it," said the Old Hermit. "When the Green Lady calls to you, go forward and slip the ring quickly on one of her slimy, cold fingers." "And then?" asked the prince. He was brave usually but he was not keen on meeting a sly lady who turned into a monster.'

Denny stopped there. 'There isn't much more,' he said. 'But it's the exciting part coming up next.' Everybody waited tensely, eager for the high spot of the story.

Denny went on—'The Old Hermit spoke—"When you slip on the ring, the Green Lady will change and the Monster will try to get free from your power. But he will disappear in a puff of smoke!" "Truly?" "Truly, my dear Prince. Only you can defeat the Monster because you broke the spell on me by giving me your last crust of bread." "Oh well, then," said the prince, standing up. "Off I go and get it over with. That Monster must be a real nuisance."

'The prince, blazing with gold and jewels, waded into the river, squinting his eyes at the mist as if looking for a place where he could cross. Suddenly, the green light formed over the water and the shape of the Green Lady came into view. She held out her arms and, smiling charmingly, called sweetly—"Walk towards me, Prince! I will help you to cross the river!" The prince went forward, gulping down his fear of the green apparition which seemed to be so beautiful and kind.

'The Green Lady held out her hands to him, dripping wet with silvery mud and slippery seaweed. "Another step forward, dear Prince!" The prince took one more step and then—quick as a flash—he slid the ring over the Green Lady's middle finger. As he did so, she screeched a dreadful cry of torment. Her head grew the horrible gnashing fangs and purple eyes and her body became covered in scales until she was in her true shape—the shape of the Monster! The wicked creature wrenched and bit at the ring which was now fastened on one long claw but it would not budge. It held firm no matter how the Monster struggled. Not moving a muscle as the teeming waters almost deluged him, the prince stared in horror at the dreadful sight as the Monster lurched and snarled. Then, with one last terrible "Argh-g-grughh! . . ." the Monster was struck by a bolt of lightning and vanished in an explosion of evil-smelling smoke.

"Hooray!" cried the Old Hermit, leaping with joy, as much as his age would allow. "You have rid us of the Monster of the Magic Pool, good Prince!"

"Henceforth—" said the prince, "henceforth, everybody shall cross the river in perfect safety. Thanks are due to you, too, Old Hermit, for without your magic ring and good advice, the Monster would still enjoy his reign of terror. I shall send you a golden staff to hold aloft as a sign to all travellers that you are their guide."

'They patted each other on the back and then all the fishermen, who had watched from a safe distance, rowed their boats swiftly towards the Magic Pool. The water was still and smooth again and the men had no fear any longer. They shouted and laughed and waved happily to the prince and the Hermit. One of the boats was rowed to the bank and the prince stepped into it. Before he sat down, he handed his golden, jewelled crown to the Old Hermit. "Share these riches amongst all who have suffered because of the Monster. I do not know how you put up with it for so long."

'The prince settled himself in the boat and was rowed across the river to the other side, with many cheerful goodbyes to the Old Hermit. Afterwards, the people in that part of Wales, on both sides of the River Taff, rejoiced and lived long and happy lives. Never more did they tremble at the thought of the Green Lady and her other self, the Monster. The Magic Pool, though, remains there to this very day for all to see. Whether it really goes down and down without end, nobody knows but sometimes the water circles strangely, to remind people of the dreadful happenings there in ages gone by. The End.'

There was a little silence before Louise said softly, 'Wow! That's brilliant, Denny.'

Feeling exhausted after so much reading, Denny folded up his notebook and looked shy. Everybody smiled and murmured praise and they all clapped to congratulate Denny on his story.

'Well done, Denny!' said Rob. 'It's all there. Our play! We'll write parts for the characters in the story, work out the action, bring in the swirling pool and so on.'

Helen Harris was delighted, too. 'A terrific effort, Denny!'

'You mean—you mean we're going to use my story for our production?'

'Certainly! It has everything. Suspense, action, sadness, joy. Yes—we'll do it!'

'But—it didn't happen. It's all out of my head,' Denny said with concern.

'That's called fiction,' said Helen. 'Most legends were stories made up to entertain people sitting around the fire long ago. No television, radio or books in those days. Almost none of the legends *really* happened but they *might* have happened.'

'It's a lovely story, Denny.' It wasn't often that Emma spoke in a serious, generous way. She wasn't sneering or sulking and Denny realised that his story had captured her imagination.

'Emma—try for the part of the Green Lady!'

'Oh, no . . . I don't think I'm good enough . . .'

''Course you are!'

'Okay, everybody! Dance routine!' Rob switched on the tape-recorder and everybody copied his movements in time to the music. The room was alive with enthusiasm. The Taff Stage Group had chosen their play, they knew where they were going and they bounced with energy and confidence.

5

On Monday, Denny had a successful day at school. He enjoyed maths and his contribution to the Population Survey, a project which Mrs Howells set for the class at the start of term. He was light-hearted as he parted from Ben and walked down Owen Street.

Before he could cross the road, the door of Number 6 opened and a pointy old face looked out.

'Denny! Your Nana's here in my house. Come in. And wipe your feet!'

It was Mrs Morris, the neighbour with the telephone. Clearly, children were not her favourite species. Denny felt like a grubby pest, crawling out of a mouldy heap. His mood altered.

'She's in there!' Mrs Morris gave Denny a shove in the direction of the kitchen. The plan of the house was exactly the same as Nana's but Mrs Morris had dingy walls and solid old-fashioned furniture. Brass candlesticks, a doleful clock and a pair of mournful china dogs stood and sat on the mantlepiece. There was a pungent smell of wax polish and disinfectant. Obviously, Mrs Morris never danced around *her* kitchen. It was the kind of room where nobody would even dare to smile.

Nana was sitting near the meagre coal fire and patting at her eyes with a pink paper tissue. Mrs Morris—severe in a black skirt and grey blouse—sat down on a high-backed chair and Denny balanced uneasily on the edge of the sofa next to Nana. Nana said—'Hello, love'—and dabbed away more tears.

'So . . . how did she look?' Mrs Morris folded her hands in her lap and fixed Nana with beady eyes.

'Well—she—she's still in bed. Her arm was fractured in the fall. Her face is bruised and there's a cut over one eye. She had seven stitches.'

Denny remembered that Nana had gone again to visit her friend in hospital. Mrs Morris wanted to hear the details.

'Did they catch him?'

Nana shook her head. 'No. He grabbed her bag and ran off. My poor—'

'Be careful what you say!' Mrs Morris snapped. 'His ears are flapping.'

Denny felt awkward and annoyed with Mrs Morris for talking about him as if he were a spy. He couldn't make any sense of what they were saying, anyway. They seemed to be speaking in a strange code.

'Nobody else saw what happened. She—she can't be moved for a week or so,' whispered Nana.

'It takes time. Shock, mostly, I expect.' Mrs Morris was relishing the conversation about the person covered in bandages at the hospital.

'Well, Denny, we must go home. Thank you, Mrs Morris.' Nana and Denny stood up.

Mrs Morris saw them out of the house. 'Use the phone any time,' she said, her face as acid as lemon juice.

Denny guessed that Mrs Morris liked hearing about other people's misfortunes but Nana was really grateful to her. He had seen the new box of chocolates in its shop bag on Mrs Morris's table. Oh, well. Perhaps he was wrong about her. People with prune faces who were impatient with children might be good and kind. Sorting out grown-ups was difficult, Denny thought. You had to take it slowly and learn who was a goodie and who was a baddie. Somebody who *appeared* to be nice and friendly might turn out to be a Big Nasty—like the Green Lady . . . Yes, grown-ups had to be thought about very carefully.

'Come on, dreamy!' said Nana, unlocking the front door. It was almost dark in the street and Denny could hardly see past the end house on the row. But he saw enough to make out the figure which dodged out of sight.

'Nana! It's that man!'

'What man?' Nana looked where Denny pointed.

'I've seen him before! He's hiding behind the end house!'

Nana frowned. 'Let's go and see!'

She marched Denny to the corner house and looked into the darkness of the side lane. There was nobody to be seen but in the gathering darkness somebody could have hidden in one of the back doorways. They waited for a few minutes and then went home.

'You didn't imagine it, Denny?'

'No, Nana. Honest.' This time he had the impression of a long dark coat, an upturned collar and pulled-down cap so that the man's face was hidden.

'And you've seen this man before?'

'Yes, Nana. Twice. Once—once over the tide and the second time I—I think he was at the market.'

Nana was angry at this. 'Why didn't you tell me?'

Denny shrugged. 'I don't know. I—I thought I might be making a mistake. Oh—and another time—over the tide—I thought I heard somebody call out.' Denny's words trailed off miserably. 'Then—just now—I'm sure it was the same man. It's all a bit of a muddle.'

Nana said, 'Always tell me about anything suspicious or scary. A false alarm is better than telling nobody and putting yourself and others at risk. I'll have to report this.'

'Yes, Nana.' Denny hung up his coat. 'I think he sleeps in that old hut by the river. Perhaps he's just a homeless person. But, Nana, why is he watching *me*?'

Nana was tight-lipped. 'We'll find out. You can't be too careful these days. I'll take you to school in the morning and meet you every afternoon.'

Denny could hardly believe his ears.

'No, Nana! I'll be all right! I'm with my friends most of the time. An' if I see the man again, I'll yell for help and run!' He didn't want to be nursemaided like a toddler. The shame of it!

'I must look after you properly, Denny. I'm responsible for you.' Nana sat down wearily. 'Oh dear—it's one problem after another.'

'It's all our fault,' Denny said gloomily. 'Me an' my Mam an' Dad. Without us you wouldn't have any worries. That's what my Mam said. We've brought you nothin' but trouble.'

Nana stared fiercely at him. 'Don't ever say that again, Denny! You and your parents are my family. No matter what happens, we'll get through the bad times!' Then she went quiet. 'I didn't know that your Mam felt like that. My poor little Trisha. She needs a lot of love just now. Nothing is going right for her.'

Denny wanted to hug Nana but he held back. The next instant Nana stood up smartly. 'Bad times don't last for ever. We have things to do. Come on—after tea you can help make some little cakes. I'll take them to the hospital tomorrow.' Later, Denny spooned creamy mixture into the paper cases. He had done this for Nana ever since he was little and he still took pride in measuring out the exact amount for a perfect cup-cake. Nana taught him other cooking, too. She said it was important. When he went away to college or to a job and lived on his own, he wouldn't starve. He licked his fingers in appreciation.

'Oh! She'll love these,' Nana murmured when she took the sweet-smelling cakes from the oven. 'I'll tell her that you made them.'

Next morning, turning a deaf ear to his complaints, Nana insisted on walking to school with Denny. She spoke with Mrs Howells, telling her about the strange man Denny had seen in the area. 'I'll be back from Newport before school comes out,' Nana promised. 'I'll be here to meet Denny.'

Mrs Howells told Mrs Jones, the School Secretary and Mrs Jones told the Headmaster. Sir then told the whole school about the man. Denny wondered what he had started. A policeman was seen walking about outside the school all morning and a policewoman took over from him in the afternoon.

71

'Ay, Denny! Is it about that tramp in the old hut over the tide?' Jayce asked.

'Yeah. I've seen him again. He's sort of followin' me around.'

'Cor!'

Lessons went well again. Denny felt more at ease, knowing that so many people were now aware of the stranger. Somehow, he sensed that the mysterious man meant him no harm but, as Nana said, it was wrong to take risks. Better safe than sorry.

After two days there was no sign of anybody lurking about and a policeman—Sergeant Evans—called at the house and spoke with Denny.

'Keep your eyes open, there's a good lad. Let us know at once if you see him again.'

Denny promised. On the following day he would be ten years old but in many ways he felt older. He had learnt quickly to endure disappointments and to make the best of what he had. He liked living with Nana but kept a calm hope that some day he would be with his Mam and Dad again.

He felt wiser than Jayce and happier than Emma. A lot had happened when he was only nine . . . What he wanted most, now, was to know that his parents were safe and well. His trust in them was strong. Times were difficult but, in his heart, he was certain that they would not fail him.

In bed that night, Denny's thoughts stopped him sleeping. His age would soon be in double figures for the first time. A milestone birthday. No party, not this year. He told Nana he was getting too big for parties, anyway; the peculiar combination of jelly, custard and sausages on sticks and the ritual of outgrown party games ... Had he been asleep, instead of letting his thoughts run on, he would not have heard the click of the letter-box and the soft thud on the passage mat. He listened more intently. All quiet. Dark and quiet. Nana was in her room and fast asleep. No sound from there. But something had been pushed through the front door ... Denny's curiosity overpowered him. He had to go downstairs to see what it was. Slowly, he stepped down the stair carpeting, his bare toes gripping the smooth strands of the pile. Once or twice he stopped, not wanting to disturb Nana. She'd think the house was being burgled! She might scream and wake up the whole street! Stealthily, Denny crept down ... then along the narrow passage. No light filtered in, not even from the street lamp. On reaching the front door Denny had to kneel and slide his hands around the floor to find the object he had heard drop. He pushed something solid, then his two hands grasped it. Corners. A small box. No. A book! Through the thin paper wrapping his fingers made out the familiar shape. He sat for a minute in the black warmth of the passage-way, holding the package to his chest. A book. But who would deliver a book in the middle of the night? Definitely not the postman.

And was the book for Nana? Or for him? Holding it tightly, Denny went noiselessly upstairs again. He turned on the bedside lamp. The book was wrapped in a piece of flimsy brown paper on which was printed one word—DENNY. His fingers started to break the wrapping, then he hesitated. It had appeared in an unusual way and he had promised Nana and the policeman that he would tell about anything suspicious ... But once again, his curiosity was greater than his caution and he tore at the rest of the paper.

He unwrapped an old book with faded dark blue covers and gold-leaf lettering which had flaked and lost its brightness. The title, though, was clear enough—'Ancient Legends of Wales'. Fantastic! A birthday present? Yes, it must be ... But who— Denny opened the book. Pencilled inside the front cover was '25p'—but nothing more. No 'To dear Denny' or 'Happy birthday from' ... Another mystery.

'Denny! Are you all right?' Nana was awake, calling out in concern.

'Yes, thanks, Nana! I'm fine!' Denny placed the book on the table next to his bed and snapped off the light. Time enough tomorrow to discuss it with Nana. But *who*—? Somebody who knew the kind of books he liked and somebody who also knew about his birthday ... As he drifted off to sleep at last, Denny desperately wanted the book to be from a certain, special person. But, of course, he knew *that* was impossible.

At breakfast, Nana wished him 'a happy birthday, lovely boy!' and presented him with a set of long-range binoculars complete with carrying case, strap and polishing cloth.

'They're incredible, Nana!' he laughed. 'Aww! Thanks!' He tried them out, focussing on things in the kitchen but all he saw was a blur.

'You need to be outside with those,' Nana said. 'Better not take them to school, though. Look, love. More cards. One from Swansea—that's from Auntie Dilys, I expect—and this one has a Gwent postmark. That'll be from Auntie Brenda in Chepstow!' They were his Nana's aunties and very, very old but they always remembered him. Auntie Dilys had written 'Penblwydd hapus i ti' as she always did. He could read and understand that sentence in Welsh. Auntie Brenda had sent a red birthday badge with a white '10' on it. He ignored this tactfully and slid it out of sight.

Nana put another card next to his plate. 'Your Mam sent this the other day. I kept it for you.'

His mother had written 'Happy Birthday to my Denny—see you soon—love and a big kiss from Mam' on a postcard showing a view of Newport Castle. Not a big grand castle—a few old bits of ruins—but it was nice to have it. The writing straggled across the card as if Mam had not held the pen properly. She usually formed her letters neatly and firmly . . . 'Your Mam will give you a present when she sees you, love,' said Nana.

'Is she coming home soon, then?' Denny re-read his Mam's card.

'Yes, she is. Now eat up. It's a bitterly cold morning.'

At school, Nana left him at the gate and Denny met up with Jayce and Emma. He told them about the binoculars and the card from his mother. He said nothing, though, about the old book appearing mysteriously at dead of night. Because breakfast had been a rush he had still not told Nana. Meanwhile, the book was secure in his jacket pocket, the brown paper folded around it.

After Morning Assembly, Sir announced that Miss Harris would like to see all the children who were in the Taff Stage Group. They were to stay in the hall and keep quiet.

'What's this about?' asked Jayce.

'Dunno,' said Emma, 'but we'll soon find out.'

Helen Harris appeared with a sheaf of papers in her arms. 'Hello, everybody! To save time, Rob Bevan and I have worked on Denny's Magic Pool story and made a little play out of it. I'd like a brief word with you first, Denny.'

Denny and Helen stood apart from the others. 'We've made a few changes, Denny. If you don't agree, then we'll talk about it. As the author of the story, you can change action or script if we've gone wrong.'

'I'll read it, Miss. I'm sure it'll be great.'

'Well—you might want to raise some points. Sure you don't mind that we've gone ahead and adapted it already?'

'No, Miss! I don't know how to write a play. I want to learn that next.'

Helen was pleased and called out—'Everybody take a copy. Read it and try for a part at Saturday's meeting. Right?'

'Right!' said everybody.

'Rob and I are composing a few songs so be prepared to learn those as well!'

Denny, Jayce, Emma and Ben went into a huddle with their scripts. 'It looks great!' said Jayce. 'Don't suppose I'll get a part, though.'

'Why not?' Emma said, teasing him. 'You can be the Monster. He doesn't say anythin'. He just looks ugly and snarls!'

'Uhh . . . funny-funny . . .' said Jayce. Then he said—'On second thoughts—thanks, Emma! That's not a bad idea!'

Denny riffled through the pages. He intended to try for the part of the Very Rich Prince but he did not like to say so to the others. For him, Saturday could not dawn too quickly.

Helen Harris said—'If you don't get a named part, there's plenty more to do. We'll need lots of fishermen and river-sprites and people helping with props. Now—do you know anybody who would help make the costumes? Somebody clever at sewing?'

Nana would help! Denny knew that she would. But it was polite to ask her first before putting her name forward. He told Helen that he would ask at home and others said the same.

'Good! Off you go to your classrooms! And don't lose your scripts!' Helen ordered.

The rest of the day went very well. Denny had a birthday card signed by Mrs Howells and everybody in his class and he had more to look forward to after school. But he was not looking forward to telling Nana about the mystery book.

'*In the middle of the night*?' Nana shrieked. 'Let me see that!'

Denny handed over the book and wrapping paper.

'H'm. Well. It *looks* harmless. But why did it arrive under cover of darkness? I'm not happy about it, Denny.'

'It's a good book, Nana. Am I allowed to keep it?'

'We'll see. So that was why your light was on late. You should have told me at once!'

'But Nana—you were fast asleep. When you woke up—whoever it was had gone—'

'How do you know? Suppose he broke in? Ohh!'

The thought panicked Nana and she threw the book aside as if it were red hot.

'Might not be a "he". Might be "she",' Denny suggested.

'It was that man!' Nana's voice was rising again.

'Yes . . . I suppose so. But Nana—how does he know that I like reading legends?'

'He has ways of finding out! Tomorrow morning I'm taking that book to Sergeant Evans. He might find fingerprints and things.' Denny had never seen Nana look so stern. He hoped fervently that Sergeant Evans would return the book when he had finished looking for clues.

'Yes. You'll have to report it.' Most of Denny's birthday had passed off pleasantly. And now there was a cake with ten candles and his name on it. It was a pity to end the day in ructions like this. He would go to bed early. The play script waited in his room.

'Nana—I might want to read out loud this evening. Sort of talking to myself. Okay?'

She didn't lift an eyebrow. 'Yes, love. I won't mind. I'm past being surprised at *anything*.'

Perhaps it wasn't the best moment to mention sewing costumes for the drama group but Denny took a chance and asked.

He need not have worried. Nana's frowns disappeared. She was ready for action. Too much action, as it turned out. 'Of course I'll help! Lovely! I'll see Miss Harris about it. Tell you what—I'll come with you to the Planet tomorrow afternoon. I'm not letting you out of my sight from now on!'

Next morning, Owen Street loomed magnificently through the binoculars, every stone and brick standing out in sharp detail. Denny watched the man with the trilby hat leave his house, his face enlarged enough to show spiky hairs bristling on his nose. Denny zoomed away to the front bedroom window of Number Six from where Mrs Morris, busy polishing with a yellow duster, gave him one of her fiercest glares. He moved down quickly, spotting an old dog trotting along the pavement.

'Denny! Come in off that doorstep! Don't stand there looking at everybody!'

Denny obeyed. It was a nuisance, being banned from going over the tide. Nana had even stopped him going to the Community Centre alone. The street was interesting in a way but it had far less appeal than the windy, muddy shoreline of the river mouth. But he had another option. Upstairs, at his bedroom window, he focussed the lenses on the back-to-back gardens between Owen Street and Treherbert Street. Most of them were not gardens in the proper sense. In some, the whole space was taken up by flat-roofed kitchen extensions. Bushes struggled for survival here and there in other yards but only one was a real little garden, where climbing plants bordered a half-moon of grass and a white seat stood on a patio of crazy-paving.

He zoomed into the middle distance, giving the booby prize for squalid untidiness to a Treherbert Street yard about half-way along the block. Part of an iron bed-frame sprawled against an old-fashioned mangle, its sagging wooden rollers eaten away by time and weather. A rusty bucket, handle missing, lay toppled near the door of an abandoned chicken-coop, its wire front crumpled and bashed in. A paint-daubed square of tarpaulin, propped against a roughly-made overhang, gave sparing protection to some old pieces of furniture. A vivid glint of electric blue contrasted jarringly with the rust, dust and decay.

What a sad, creepy place! But what was that—? He swung the angle of vision downwards again. Yes. There it was. That flash of bright blue. Denny increased the magnification and looked carefully, holding the binoculars steady. It was! Certain of his discovery, he dashed from the room, belting down the stairs. Hurling himself towards the front door, he flung it open—

'Denny! Where are you going?'

'Round to Jayce's! I'll be all right!'

'Denny! Come back here!'

But Denny had already gone. Holding the binoculars in front of him he ran the few short blocks to Jayce's house. Jayce saw him before he reached the door.

'What d'you want? It's too early for Norton Street!'

'I know that. You must come with me, Jayce. There's something you have to see!'

Jayce looked doubtful. 'See *what*? I'm not going over the tide-field . . .'

'No! You can see this from Nana's house. Honest! Jayce . . . I think I've found your bike!'

Jayce's jaw dropped in amazement. 'Where? Are you serious—?'

'Course I'm serious! I saw it through my binoculars. Come *on*, Jayce!'

Instantly, Jayce was caught up in Denny's excitement. His bicycle had disappeared several weeks before and he had given up hope of ever seeing it again.

Nana opened the front door to them and scolded—'What *is* all this?—hello, Jason—Denny! I told you not to go out on your own! Can't you do what you're told?'

'Sorry, Nana. Come on, Jayce. Quick!'

The two boys rushed up the stairs and into Denny's room. Denny lifted the strap over his head. 'Look through the binocs. That untidy yard at the back of Treherbert Street . . . Got it?'

'Yeah . . . Sort of. I can't see much. An old bucket

'. . . a rabbit-hutch, I think . . . an' some cupboards 'n things under a kind of cover . . .'

'That's it! The old furniture. Now look carefully. See? Next to that sheet of waterproof stuff . . .'

Jayce stared through the eyes of the binoculars. 'Yeah . . . Yeah! I can see it! It's a new bike. Exactly like mine! The same colour, anyway . . . Denny— you've found it! I'm sure it's my bike!'

'Do you know who lives there?' Denny asked him.

Jayce could hardly speak. He said slowly . . . 'Yes. I know who lives there. And so do you.'

'Who?' Denny's instinct told him that Jayce had bad news.

Jayce handed back the binoculars. He looked again through the window towards the neglected backyard in Treherbert Street.

'It might not be my bike. There are hundreds of bikes that colour . . .'

'Who lives there?' persisted Denny.

'Emma Price,' said Jayce.

6

'Faster, River-sprites! Ripple the water! Good!'

Rehearsals at Norton Street were under way. Three girls—Louise was one of them—and three boys had been chosen as River-sprites. Helen Harris was showing them how to make waves with long bands of green and grey silky material. Round and round they went, creating a fabric whirlpool.

Parts had been given out after the auditions. Green Lady—Emma Price, Monster—Jason Morgan, Rich Prince—Ben Sarami, Very Rich Prince—Denny Thomas. A boy called Mark Hughes (from Emma's class) was cast as the Old Hermit. Several boys, rowing with imaginary oars, were practising to be the Fishermen. Everybody had to sing in the chorus, even those people without parts in the play.

'Have you spoken to Emma yet?' Denny asked Jayce. They were waiting to go through their parts.

'No. Dunno what to say.' Jayce, glum and uncertain, had avoided Emma since they all arrived at Norton Street. Denny, seeing how pleased she was at winning the Green Lady part, had given her a thumbs-up sign. She might know nothing about the bike. Some other person could have hidden it amongst the scrap and junk in the Price's backyard.

'Green Lady! Rich Prince!' Rob Bevan called for Emma and Ben who took up their places and read their lines from their scripts.

'Monster! Get ready to take over from the Green Lady!'

Emma sank down so that Jayce could take her place. The River-sprites circled furiously, dragging their lengths of material. Ben—caught by the Monster—yelled hoarsely. The Fishermen rowed their boats swiftly away from the scene.

'Denny! I'm going to the shops. I'll come back for you at four o'clock,' Nana whispered. Denny had forgotten that she was there. He had to admit that she had been very good, quiet as a mouse. After talking with Miss Harris about costumes, she sat out of the way in a corner.

'Okay,' he said. 'See you then.' Inwardly, relief swept over him. Nana would miss hearing him go through his part. Rehearsals would be over by the time she returned. Why was he suddenly shy? He would have to conquer that.

Rob Bevan ordered silence. 'Before we go on . . . We should have names for the two princes. We can't call them Rich and Very Rich. Names will look better on the printed programme.'

'Why not use their own names?' Helen Harris had her pen poised, ready to alter the cast list.

'My name is Benjula,' said Ben.

'That has a good sound. Prince Benjula!'

'And you, Denny? Have you another name? Prince Denny doesn't seem quite right . . .'

'Denzil. His proper name is Denzil.'

Nana had spoken from the doorway. Denny felt his knees go weak. His secret . . . his terrible secret . . . was out. He had always pushed his real name into the far corner of his mind, almost believing that he was simply 'Denny'. But now . . . Now they all knew the shaming truth.

Nobody said a word until Helen Harris broke the unbearable quiet. 'Denzil! Why didn't you tell us that your name is Denzil?'

Denny went all colours. He started to stammer excuses.

'Speak up, Denny!' said Nana. 'You know what children are,' she smiled at Miss Harris. 'They never like their names, do they? He was named after his grandfather, my dear husband. Well—I'll be back later.'

The damage done, Nana gave a little wave and tripped away down the steps About a century seemed to pass before anybody spoke.

'Denzil! Prince Denzil! It's perfect. Sort of—noble,' Emma said and the others murmured approval.

Denny gulped. They liked it? 'You—really think it's all right?'

'Great! Well—let's get on, shall we?' Rob Bevan called for the Fishermen to assemble. Denny relaxed. Nobody had even smirked at his name. An astounding fact. Why had he ever had a moment's qualm? Denzil was a good name! A good old proud name!

'Prince Denzil! Cross stage to the Fishermen! Cue for song right there but skip that for today—go on with your lines! Remember your *breathing.* No tight jaws, please!'

Denny went through his paces, enjoying himself immensely.

PRINCE DENZIL: Good fishermen! Ferry me over the great River Taff! Here are jewels! Here is gold!

FISHERMEN (mumbling in fear as they row away) Rhubarb, rhubarb, rhubarb . . .

PRINCE DENZIL: Oh—woe is me! (He puts a fist to his forehead in despair) What ails them? Will no one help me to cross these waters?

'Right! Stop there!' called Rob. 'The big scene between Prince Denzil and the Old Hermit is next. Stand by—Green Lady, Monster, Sprites and Fishermen!'

Three old chairs lay on their sides on the floor, forming three sides of the Old Hermit's hut. The Old Hermit (Mark) was scrunched up into a corner, Helen Harris's cardigan (representing rags) over his head and shoulders. 'Okay, Prince Denzil! Begin!'

PRINCE DENZIL: (sitting down with a weary sigh) I am faint with hunger. (He opens his belt-pouch) Only a crust of bread . . . Oh—why did I not buy

fish from the fishermen? They are gone now! Well . . .
I shall save the crust until I can bear my hunger no
more. (He stands and looks towards the hut) Ah!
I see a dismal dwelling yonder in the mist. Even a
poor peasant might have a boat or a coracle for hire.
(He walks across stage and looks into the hut)
Nothing! Nobody! Only a heap of murky rags . . .

OLD HERMIT (shaking and speaking in a cracked voice)
E-eh E-eh?

At this point, there was a shout of laughter from the
others.

'Hush—shh!' Rob held up his hands, stopping
them. 'Again, Old Hermit!'

OLD HERMIT: Eh? Who is that? Who wishes to speak
with a miserable object like me?

PRINCE DENZIL: (aside) Oh! Arms and legs thinner
than a grasshopper's! An old . . . old man . . .
Half-starved, by the look of him. Oh . . . pity fills
my heart. (He speaks to the Old Hermit) Sir!
Forgive my boldness but—you are in a sorry
plight. When did you last eat any food?

OLD HERMIT: Food? (remembering) Ah . . . food
. . . I cannot remember exactly when I ate last.
Years ago, I think . . .

PRINCE DENZIL: You poor old man! Take this crust.
(He takes the crust from the belt-pouch) It is all I

have but you are welcome to it. When I cross the river I shall return with tasty morsels for you.

(The OLD HERMIT reaches out with a shaky arm to take the crust. Then he chews on it hungrily. As he finishes, gulping down the last crumb, he begins to change, his limbs growing firm and strong, his head standing proudly on his shoulders.)

PRINCE DENZIL: Ohh! He alters before my eyes! What weird magic is this?

OLD HERMIT: One act of kindness had the power to give me strength, O Prince! The Green Lady of the Magic Pool put a spell on me many years ago. Until your crust of bread restored me to the pink of condition, I was doomed to crawl about, a weak old crackly bag of bones . . .!

PRINCE DENZIL: This is a mighty wonder! But—what Magic Pool? And who is the Green Lady? She sounds very nasty.

Rob Bevan shouted—'Okay! Stop it there! Five minutes' break! Good work, cast!'

Denny and Mark were surrounded. 'Terrific! Brill! Great!'

'A lot of work to be done yet . . .' Denny said modestly—and Mark amused everybody by doing his ragged-old-man voice.

'Honest, Denny—it's going to be great,' said Emma. 'Was I okay?'

'Yeah! Sure! You and Jayce do a smooth change-over from Green Lady to Monster. That's difficult.'

Emma moved a little closer to him. 'Denny—can I speak to you—er—so that the others don't hear?'

Denny swallowed and nodded. Here was a chance to challenge Emma about the bike but he did not have that kind of courage. They went over to stand near the radiator and pretended to compare notes on their scripts.

'What's on your mind, Emma?'

'Not sure. I mean—well—it's Jayce! He's sort of . . . gone funny.'

'Oh yeah?'

'Yeah. He won't speak to me—or even look at me!'

'Oh! Ohh . . . I expect he's busy thinking about his moves and lines in the play.'

Emma turned down her mouth. 'He's talkin' to the others. Look at him! An' I saw him talkin' to *you*.'

'Mmm. Well . . . I mean—there is something—'

'What? What have I done? I thought we were all friends.'

'We were—We *are*! Oh, Emma—you'll have to talk to Jayce. I can't handle this.'

To Denny's dismay, Emma's eyes filled with tears. She did not need to say that she loved being part of a group of friends and wanted nothing to spoil it. Without words, Denny sensed her feelings.

'Emma—*don't*! Listen . . . Jayce and I will see you after rehearsals. We'll talk about it then.'

'Places, everybody!'

Denny and Jayce exchanged meaningful glances. Denny hissed—'Stay around for a few minutes after rehearsal!'

The cast worked on their moves and lines to the end of the play. Rob said 'Curtain!' and looked at his watch. 'Ten past four! Mr Hopkins will be here at any minute! Pack up, kids! No scripts next week. Everybody must be word perfect!' There was a groan.

Just then, Nana arrived laden with groceries, fruit and vegetables. Rob and Helen watched anxiously for Mr Hopkins.

'Do you want to leave?' Nana asked them. 'I'll wait for Mr Hopkins. I know him well.'

'Very kind of you, Mrs Lewis,' Helen Harris said. 'It would help. Rob and I have another appointment before five o'clock.'

'You go on, then. Now—have all the children gone? Oh, no . . .'

'It's all right, Nana. Jayce an' Emma an' me want to have a sort of—um—meeting.'

'Jayce and Emma and *I* . . .' Helen Harris corrected him but Rob said—'Oh—let's get away, Helen. Thanks, Mrs Lewis! Sure you don't mind? See you!' They were gone in a flash.

Nana said—'Mr Hopkins is very late.'

'Yes. He's fussy about us gettin' out by four o'clock usually.' Emma frowned with a hint of her old scowling surliness.

'I'll pop over the road and see where he is,' said Nana. 'Now don't get up to mischief, you children. And don't leave here without me. I'll be back in five minutes.'

As soon as she was gone, Emma said—'Okay, then. What's upsetting you, Jason Morgan?'

'*Me*?'

'Don't pretend. You've been lookin' at me as if I'm poison!'

'Oh. Oh, well—you might as well know, Emma. It's about my bike.'

Emma paled. 'Y-your bike? Well, what about it?' For an instant, the sullen aggressive girl appeared again.

Denny said—'I saw a bike—like the one Jayce lost—in your backyard, Emma. I was trying out my new binocs and I saw it—pushed in by some old furniture.'

Emma began to twist her hands together, her face embarrassed and fearful. 'I didn't—I never—'

'Look, Emma—if somebody else in your family pinched it, then tell them to give it back. I won't make any trouble,' Jayce promised.

Emma spoke in a half whisper, almost to herself . . . 'There's only my Mam an' my Gran an' me. Gran almost never leaves her bed an' Mam's got arthritis 'cos the house is so cold. Since—since my Dad died, everything sort of—went to pieces. The house an' the backyard—an' everything . . .'

Denny looked at Jayce. It sounded as if Emma was battling through life more or less on her own.

'I took it. I took the bike. From outside the Community Centre. I didn't know it was yours, Jayce.'

A moment's awkwardness followed her confession.

'What are you goin' to do about me? I stole it.'

Jayce avoided answering. 'Dad had my name engraved on the frame in a secret place—so that'll prove it's mine . . . Just so that there's no mistake.'

Denny added—'Yes—that's where Jayce left it—outside the Centre.'

Emma was still concerned about her fate. 'But—will you tell on me? You should. But—will you?'

Jayce though for half a second. 'No,' he said. 'We'll come around to collect it, okay?'

Denny could not hold back the question—'Emma—*why*? Why did you do it?'

Emma shrugged her shoulders. 'Dunno. I can't even ride a bike. But—there it was. Blue an' shining new an'—well—it's no excuse but—I didn' have anythin' much goin' for me. An' I took it.'

'You've plenty going for you now,' Denny said. 'Give Jayce his bike and then we can all be friends again.'

The anguish lifted from Emma eyes. 'That's all? That's *it*? Ohh . . . thank goodness. I promise you— I've never stolen anything else—before or since. I'm sorry, Jayce. I'm not a thief. But—I tell lies. My Mam's not an actress.'

'Oh—we knew *that*. Who cares?' said Denny. 'Oh!—look out. Here's Nana. And Mr 'Opkins!'

Nana was talking nineteen to the dozen.

'Here we are!' Nana called. 'Mr Hopkins fell asleep in front of the fire. Didn't you, Oppo?'

He was so rumpled and crumpled that he might have been asleep for six months but he blinked his dozy eyes awake and gave Nana a cheerful smile. 'It's a real treat to see you. Remember the good old days?'

'Don't I just! I'd like a pound for every time we twirled around this floor, Oppo.'

'You kids sit down and wait!' Mr Hopkins said. He ushered Nana to the end of the room and the mound of objects under the threadbare cover. 'Let me show you what's 'ere, Bronwen.'

It was a shock to Denny to hear Nana called by her first name. The three children watched as Mr Hopkins lifted a large black box and set it on a table. 'See what this is, Bron? This'll bring back a few memories!'

'Oh! Oppo! The old wind-up gramophone! And records!'

'Aye! All 'ere like it was yesterday, my lovely. What about this one—ay? *La Paloma*!'

94

Nana jumped with excitement. 'My favourite tango!'

Mr Hopkins wound a handle on the side of the box. The lid stood open, revealing a worn purple velvet lining, a turn-table and a sort of curved arm which slid over onto the old record.

'There's a needle in it,' said Mr Hopkins. He set the needle in the groove of the black disc and a soft, scratchy melody filled the room.

'Rrr-um tum, tum, tum—darum, darum, dum— Drr-um tum, tum, tum—' sang Mr Hopkins.

'Oh, Oppo—it's lovely!'

'May I have this dance, Bronwen?'

'With pleasure, Oppo.'

In time to the sultry music, Nana and Mr Hopkins began the dips, sudden turns and hesitations of the tango. They danced elegantly, as if giving an exhibition. Nana's chin was held high, her back arched gracefully, although she was wearing her old mac and tweed skirt. Mr Hopkins somehow rose above his shabby clothes and flip-flop slippers as he guided her around the floor. The exotic strains of the tango music, played by some long-forgotten orchestra, transported Denny to cowboy films on the television. Mr Hopkins became a Mexican gaucho, performing the strange, sinuous dance in high-heeled boots, baggy pants and a bolero. Nana was a liquid-eyed Spanish lady, frilled and fringed in a hundred dazzling colours. Denny could almost smell the blossoms in her hair. Mr Hopkins swerved so that Nana leaned backwards and forwards, then off they went in a run of little steps, keeping perfect time to the beat. The children could not take their eyes off the dancers.

'Aw! I wish I could tango like that,' breathed Emma.

'Ee-yuk, ee-yuk, ee-yuk, ee-yuk . . .' Suddenly, the music hiccuped on two notes.

'Needle's stuck,' said Nana. The room returned to normal. Mr Hopkins stopped the turntable and Nana picked up her shopping.

'Nice to see you, Oppo. Thanks for the dance. You'd better hurry or you'll miss the Football Results. Come along, children.'

The four kept together in the street, the children helping Nana to carry the bags.

'Jayce and I have to go to Emma's house, Nana, to—um—collect something.'

'I'll go with you.' Denny looked helpless. He couldn't escape from Nana these days.

Emma's mother had lank hair and dull skin, as if she hadn't been out in the fresh air for ages. Her hands were curled against her droopy cardigan and she walked slowly and with difficulty. Nana looked into the unswept front passage.

'Oh. Hello,' said Emma's mother.

Emma pushed past her. 'Jayce's bike is here. I'm going to get it.'

Emma's mother asked no questions, behaving as if she had no energy for anything outside her pain. While Emma was gone, Denny and Jayce stood about without speaking. Nana rested the shopping bags on the pavement. Mrs Price did not invite them into the house.

Nana said kindly—'Don't stand at the door, Mrs Price. You're not well.' Mrs Price turned and withdrew slowly into a side room.

'Poor soul. No age at all and twisted up with arthritis,' said Nana. 'Emma took your bike, did she, Jason?'

Denny's eyes popped. Nana couldn't be fooled.

'It's okay, ' said Jayce. 'Please don't say anything, Mrs Lewis. It's all sorted out now. I don't want to make trouble for Emma.'

'She needs friends,' said Nana. 'I think she's found some good ones.'

Emma reappeared, wheeling the gleaming blue bicycle through the passage. Jayce welcomed it like a long-lost friend. In the gathering dusk, it seemed little worse for the long weeks spent out of doors. Jayce found his name on the frame.

'See?' he said to Emma.

She did not look for the proof. 'I believe you,' she said.

Jayce had no lights so he proudly pushed his bicycle away, postponing a ride until next day.

At home, Denny looked at a comic and then helped Nana in the kitchen. He yawned. What a day!

'Sleepy head—time for bed!' chanted Nana.

'It's early, Nana!'

'Well, we have a big day ahead of us tomorrow.'

'Doing what?'

'I—er—I have to go to Newport again. To the hospital.'

'*Again*?'

'Yes. But this might be the last time. When I come home, I'll probably have a big surprise for you.'

'What kind of surprise?'

'A nice one. The best surprise you could possibly have.'

'But—while you're gone—what will happen to *me*?'

Nana looked uncomfortable. Then, all in a rush, she said—'I hope you don't mind, Denny, but I've arranged for you to stay with Mrs Morris.'

'*Mrs Morris*? At Number Six?' It was like doom descending on him.

Nan nodded. 'Be a good boy and help me out. It's only for a few hours. I'll be home before you know it.'

Denny was flabbergasted. He spoke grumpily—'Aww . . . Nana . . . Do I have to?'

'Now listen, Den. I have some savings for a rainy day, so I'm going to have a taxi there and back. I might be away a lot less than two hours.'

'Can't I go with you, Nana? Newport! We might see my Mam!'

'Yes—well—it's more difficult than that. Denny—I can't explain, love. Trust me to do the right thing, there's a good boy. You can help me most of all by staying with Mrs Morris.'

Denny turned away, sulking. 'Huh . . . That'll be a laugh a minute!'

'Denny! *What* did you say? Mrs Morris is a very nice lady. When you know more about—everything—you'll realise how kind to us she is.'

Denny wasn't giving up that easily. 'Can't I stay with Jayce?'

'No, you can't. Mrs Morgan has more than enough to do, looking after her own three children, without bothering about you as well!'

'But I wouldn't *be* any bother!'

'Denny! Don't argue, love. You're giving me a headache. I promise you that tomorrow will most likely turn out to be very special. Just do this one little thing for me. Please.'

The prospect of Mrs Morris's gloomy house was horrible. In his mind, Denny could hear the sad tick-tock of the carved kitchen clock and he could see Mrs Morris's old prune face glaring at him. He would have to sit there and *suffer*, not daring to move or say a word. Two hours of misery. He thought of those unhappy china dogs on the mantlepiece. Poor things. He knew what they were going through.

'Come on—cheer up! Two hours won't last for ever, Denny!'

'Well . . . I s'pose I'll have to stay with Old Prune Fa—Mrs Morris. I don't want to, though.'

Nana tried to look pleased but Denny could see that she was disappointed. She had expected him to be more willing to help. All at once, he was deeply ashamed and sorry. Nana was so good to him. She shared everything she had, she made jokes and, when things went wrong, she picked up the pieces. Then the first time she asked him to do something for *her,* he was all grumps and sulks.

'Sorry, Nana. 'Course I'll stay with Mrs Morris. I'll be safe there 'til you get back.'

Nana sighed with relief. 'There's my lovely boy! Off you go, then. Have a nice bath—and you can read in bed.'

Propped up against his pillows, Denny made a really ugly face at the thought of Mrs Morris's depressing house and that made him feel better. Then, the idea of the two of them, himself and Old Prune Face, sitting there for hours in stony silence, made him laugh. Even if it wasn't a load of fun, a visit to Mrs Morris's house might turn out to be interesting—rather like spending the afternoon in a museum.

That evening, he had decided to write not read. Thinking so much about the Magic Pool in recent weeks had given him an idea. Magic ought to be used to do some good, he thought. He scribbled words in his notebook, the same book he had used to write the Magic Pool story. This time, though, he was trying a poem. He wrote words, crossed them out, wrote others and, at last, he was satisfied with the result. In a clear voice he read—

> Magic waters, magic pool
> Make the monster look a fool!
> Magic river, magic sea—
> Bring Mam and Dad back home to me!

Then, to represent the whirlpool, he drew three large circles in the air. 'There. That should do it,' he thought. 'No harm in trying, anyway.'

7

The taxi was booked for two o'clock next day. Fifteen minutes earlier, Denny was delivered by Nana to Mrs Morris's doorstep.

'Oh. There you are, boy!' Mrs Morris snapped. 'Have you brought those binocular things?'

Denny blinked. 'Yes.' The binocs were around his neck because he couldn't bear to be parted from them. They would be of no use whatsoever in Mrs Morris's kitchen but still he had brought them.

To his surprise, Mrs Morris said 'Good. We're going out for a walk. It's a sin to waste this good weather.'

Denny cheered up immediately. He wasn't going to be stifled in the gloomy kitchen, after all!

Mrs Morris said to Nana—'Don't worry. I'll look after him. I brought up two boys and they turned out all right.'

So Nana left him there and he waited for Mrs Morris while she went upstairs. She was down again in two minutes, wearing an itchy-looking grey coat buttoned up to her neck and a stern black hat clamped down onto her eyebrows. For a wild moment, Denny expected her to fly out of the front door on a broomstick.

'Come on then!' she ordered, grabbing her handbag from the old-fashioned hallstand. She slammed her front door and marched Denny along the street.

'Where are we going, Mrs Morris?'

'The Community Centre. You can look at the sea-birds from the upstairs windows and I can have a cup of tea.'

She stared fiercely ahead as they walked past the shops but Denny glanced at her with new respect. She had given the afternoon some thought and planned what he would like to do. He was encouraged.

'We—um—we're doing a play—sort of about the river . . .' he began.

'Humph!' huffed Mrs Morris. Oh. He had made a mistake. She was being neighbourly and helping Nana but she wasn't really interested in him. Her glare told him that plays and binoculars were all a lot of nonsense.

Soon, they were crossing the dividing road between the last houses and the tide-fields. Denny trained his binoculars on the squat shape of the Centre. Not many people about.

'You should be in Sunday School,' snapped Mrs Morris, reading his thoughts.

'I'm joining when—when we're more settled. I used to go when I was little. I liked it. Lots of good stories.'

'Yes. You can rely on the Bible for good stories. Hundreds of them. Come along! Don't dawdle!'

She walked at a cracking pace. Denny had to work hard to keep up with her. To slow her down, he asked her a question . . . 'Mrs Morris. Do you have any grandchildren?'

She slackened speed. 'Yes. Four. Two girls, two boys.'

'Where are they, then?'

'Two in America. Two in Canada. I never see any of them.'

'Never?'

'Never.' She saw Denny's shocked expression. 'I'm too old to travel. They're nearly grown up so they might visit me one day. But Owen Street isn't very exciting, is it?'

Privately, Denny thought that Owen Street was exciting enough for anybody. For the first time, though, he realised how lonely Mrs Morris must be, with her two sons and their families so far away.

'I'm sorry that you don't ever see them . . .'

'You get used to it! Here we are, my lad! Well? Hold the door open for me! Where are your manners?'

'Sorry, Mrs Morris.' Denny held the door as she passed majestically into the Centre building. They went upstairs to the Refreshment Bar and chose a table near the window.

'You can do this,' she said, taking money from her purse. 'Bring a cup of tea for me. And what would you like?'

'A Coke, please. Thank you very much.'

'Good boy. "Please" and "thank you" cost nothing .' She almost smiled—but not quite.

When they were settled with their drinks, Denny lifted the binoculars to his eyes and scanned the far bank of the river. He hardly ever saw a water-rat because they liked dark, secret places but now, sharply, he saw the flick of a grey body slip into the river. On the rough stonework retaining the steep bank, a committee of fat grey gulls met like portly aldermen on spindly legs. They surveyed the draining water with round, rapid eye-blinks.

'Ohh . . . it's great, Mrs Morris!'

'I used to stand over there—where you're looking—and wait for my father's ship to come in. He was a ship's captain.'

Denny lowered the binoculars and turned to see Mrs Morris gazing across the river and into the past. 'A sea captain? In the olden days?'

'Yes—he wore a peaked cap and brass buttons on his coat. Oh—he was a fine man, my father. He always brought presents from foreign lands.'

'What kind of presents?'

'Oh—the old things you see in my house. He brought those for my mother. He brought me dolls and toys from all over the world. I was a lucky little girl.'

A picture of Mrs Morris's kitchen flashed into Denny's mind. Perhaps Mrs Morris would tell him where the strange old things came from . . . Her face was softer, remembering. It was weird. Behind that old wrinkly face was a little girl waiting eternally for her father's ship to come home . . .

'Well! I'm going to have another cup of tea. What about you, Denny? Another whatd'ycallit?'

'No, thank you, Mrs Morris.' He raised his binoculars again, gazing along the near bank.

Suddenly, a flurry of activity brought noise and movement over the tide fields. He let the binoculars

105

fall, suspended on their strap. 'Mrs Morris! Mrs Morris! *Look!*'

Denny was pointing to a convoy of vehicles, droning, grinding and clunking over the uneven field. Trucks, earth-movers, concrete mixers, Land-Rovers . . . alien shapes and sounds, invading the peace of the river bank. '*Mrs Morris! What are they doing?*'

'Let me see through those things.'

She pulled the binoculars sideways, stretching the strap about Denny's neck and staring through the lenses at the activity in the distance.

'Riverside Construction!' she read from the sides of the lorries. She gave the binoculars back to Denny.

'What's that? Who are they?'

'They're the people who are going to build on this side of the river.'

'No! Oh, no!'

Dismayed, Denny watched the vehicles stop. Men in overalls and hard-hats jumped down, striding about in wellington boots, pointing and shouting. Two of them produced a large cylinder, unrolling a tape which they set along the ragged edge of the bank. A couple of tipper lorries began to unload their cargoes of large rubble which went crashing down into jagged heaps, belching clouds of choking dust. One of the men tramping about signalled to a truck driver. Denny watched the truck jolt forward

106

and the driver lean out and look back. 'Ohh! I hope they get swallowed up in the Magic Pool!' he shouted in rage.

'Quiet, please!' Mrs Morris chastised. 'They're only doing their work, you know.'

'Yes. I know that. But—the river—the birds—the-the Magic Pool . . .'

'I know, boy. I know. But it might be for the best.'

Denny did not believe this. He lifted the binoculars again, studying the hateful scene of busy intruders with their parade of powerful transport and machines. He looked again at the man signalling to the truck driver. Something familiar there . . . No. No, he thought. It can't be true. It can't . . . be . . . true! He looked again, trying to steady the binoculars. 'But it is true! It is! IT IS! IT IS!

'Mrs Morris!' The tense pallor of his face alarmed her.

'What on earth's the matter?'

'Mrs Morris! Come *on*! You must go to the river with me! *Please*!'

'Whatever for? Here—I haven't had my tea—'

'*Please*, Mrs Morris!'

'What's all this about? What's the matter with you, boy?'

'I can't go near the river by myself—I promised!—oh, please—it's *important*!' For the second time, the binoculars had revealed a startling sight.

It was useless to stand there pleading so Denny grabbed Mrs Morris by the arm and ran from the room, hauling her with him.

'Stop! Stop!' she cried—but down the steps and out of the main door Denny flew. Outside, he ran on ahead so that she was forced to follow. She might be a good walker but she was a hopeless runner. She puffed and panted and held onto her hat, her little fat legs pumping up and down.

'Oohh—you dreadful boy! Come back!' she shouted, gasping and wheezing. 'Oohh!'

Denny ran on and on, into the working area of the trucks and men. A burly foreman yelled at the top of his voice—'Get that kid away from here! There's heavy plant moving!'—over the din of revving engines and clanking machinery. Denny dodged and swerved, running, running . . .

Mrs Morris screamed—'Denn-eeeee! Come back here! Oohh!—wait 'til I tell your Nana!'

Denny closed his ears to Mrs Morris as he pounded over the tide-field. Nothing and nobody mattered as he pelted onwards, only one thought in his head. He had lost sight of his target but a group of men had gone farther downstream. On he ran, shouting and waving his arms . . . But—in his haste, he had forgotten the gulley, cutting into the field at a right angle to the river bank. He reached the narrow cleft before he could pull back from the edge, his speed propelling him to the opposite side of the break in the ground. Down he went with a yell of fear, his feet finding no hold but, miraculously, his stubby fingers clutching at the strong grass topping the gulley wall. The fall knocked the breath out of him, hitting his chest painfully, the binoculars slamming against his ribs like a stone. His finger-joints sought more grass in a frantic attempt to hold on but his grasp was slackening, his arms tearing from their sockets. He let out a last, desperate cry of despair, his eyes staring upwards as if searching for deliverance. His eyes closed as his hands slipped through the last blades of grass keeping him suspended above the deep mud in the blackness far below. Suddenly, two strong hands reached down, grabbing Denny's thin arms so that his weight was taken—and held.

Denny stared upwards, gazing into two vivid blue eyes the image of his own. '*Dad*! Oh—Dad!'

The moment would never leave him. He would remember it all his life, as though he stood apart watching the man rescuing the boy, the scene forever painted on his memory.

'It's all right, son. You're safe. I've got you! Slowly does it . . . up you come, now . . . '

Hoisted inch by inch, Denny drew nearer and nearer to his father. At last they stood triumphantly on the grass and Denny's Dad lifted him and swung him around with a roar of joy.

'Hello, Den! How's my boy?'

'Dad! Oh, Dad!' Denny half-sobbed, half-laughed. 'I knew it was you!' Yes, he knew it all now. The hut, the market, the book—everything.

All at once, a grey and black tornado came puffing over the field. Mrs Morris had gone to the narrowest, innermost part of the gulley and hopped over, rushing towards the reunion of father and son.

As she stumbled up to them, her handbag curved out in a mighty swing, catching Denny's Dad square on the back of his donkey-jacket.

'OW!'

'Unhand that boy!'

Wham! Her handbag struck again like a guided missile. And again—WHACK!

'Ouch! Stop it, Mrs Morris! It's me! Denny's Dad!'

Denny scrambled out of range of another swipe. Mrs Morris lunged at him, bringing him to her side. She glowered at Dad. 'I know who you are, young man! Let me inform you that Denny is in *my* charge and he goes nowhere without *my* permission!—It's bad enough that he almost fell in the river!'

Dad looked helpless. He stood there in his big boots, working clothes and hard-hat, like an overgrown boy being put in his place.

'I saw Dad through my binoculars,' said Denny. 'I thought he might go away again if I didn't stop him!'

'Humph!' said Mrs Morris. Her hat had fallen over one eye and she pushed it up impatiently. 'My orders are to take you straight back to your Nana!'

'Denny—where's your Mam?' asked Dad.

'She—she's gone away to Newport to work. Dad— you're not going back to London?'

'Definitely not. Mrs Morris—I don't want to take Denny away. I'm coming home with you to Nana's house.'

Denny, still shaken and very muddy, gazed at his Dad in wonder. His poem-wish had come true! Well—half of it, anyway. His dad *had* come back to him! It was amazing! Incredible! It was—*magic*!

'Are you all in one piece, son? No bones broken?'

'I'm okay, Dad.' Denny felt six feet tall. He made a feeble effort to brush down his clothes.

'Oh—look at you—and your Nana so particular!' fussed Mrs Morris. She tried to pull his clothes into shape but, somehow, Denny's garments always had a mind of their own.

'He's fine,' said Dad. 'Listen—I'll be off work in an hour . . .'

'We'll wait for you at the Centre,' said Mrs Morris firmly. 'We're not going back yet. Mrs Lewis has gone out.' She glared again at Denny's Dad. 'And you won't get any more from me than that. My lips are sealed!'

She's at it again, thought Denny. Talking in riddles. Like she had a big, important secret. He looked at his Dad. Dad said—'You stay with Mrs Morris, Den. I'll find you both at the Centre when I finish work.'

On the top floor of the Community Centre again, Denny was in a state of nervous excitement. He could not sit down for longer than a minute. Up he jumped again and again, going to the window, looking out, coming back to the table.

'Calm down, boy! You're a terrible fidget!'

'Aw—it's great, Mrs Morris! I can hardly believe that my Dad is really and truly back home!'

'He's home,' she said. 'And he's found a job . . . Huh! They've cleared my tea away. Well—I'm certainly not paying for any more!'

She gave Denny a disapproving look, blaming him for the wasted cup of tea. Denny, though, hardly noticed. He sank onto his chair. 'Yeah. He's found a job. But why does he have to work for *them*? Spoiling the river?'

Mrs Morris was stern. 'Work is not easy to find these days. And something needs to be done on that old river bank.'

Denny nodded. 'Yes—I know it's scruffy. But the river won't be the same . . .'

'This Centre wasn't always here. Some people didn't want it built—but it's part of the community now,' Mrs Morris reminded him.

Denny mutely accepted what she said. It didn't stop his anger; anger at the fact that the only work available for his Dad was destroying the habitat of sea-birds, water-creatures and flowers of the riverside. There would soon be a hideous, brash hotel or club where the grass once waved free in the wind.

It was strange that Denny should be discussing the fate of his beloved riverside with Mrs Morris, of all people. It proved that you never really knew what was going to happen. Mrs Morris wasn't as sympathetic a listener as Nana. Still, she heard him out with respect even though she disagreed.

'Ah, well,' she said at last. 'Life is all change. We can only hope that the changes make things better, not worse.' She checked the time with the lady at the serving hatch. 'The hour is up. We'd better wait downstairs. Your father will be here any minute.'

Dad met them at the main entrance. His hard-hat had gone but he still wore the heavy boots, overalls and jacket.

'Ready?'

'Yes, Dad.'

The three walked to Owen Street. Denny couldn't stop looking up at his father. He had the scary feeling that he might be in the middle of a dream—that he had fallen asleep with boredom in Mrs Morris's kitchen and he would wake up, his happiness shattered. But no . . . this was no dream. He was with Dad and—oddly—Mrs Morris. They were as real as the broken pavements.

'Binoculars!' Dad noticed.

'Yes. My birthday present from Nana.'

Dad smiled, amused. 'She spoils you.'

113

'Yes. I know.' Denny was on sure ground when he said—'Dad—thank you for the book.'

'I thought you'd like it, son. Sorry I couldn't afford more at the time.' Denny remembered the 25p marked inside the book cover. Poor Dad. He had been down to his last few pence—but he had remembered the birthday. Denny wondered if his Dad would get into trouble for going about in the middle of the night when—as Nana said—all respectable people were in bed asleep.

'Here we are, then!' Almost without realising it, they were in Owen Street outside Nana's bright yellow front door. Mrs Morris had taken control—for Dad seemed to be overcome with shyness—and she knocked smartly. Nana's face went pale when she opened the door and saw Denny's Dad. Then she said—'So you're back.'

'Yes. Hello, Mam. I couldn't show my face before. But I've got a job now. Sorry if I caused trouble, hanging about.'

'I'll be going,' said Mrs Morris, her duty done.

Dad said to her—'Thanks for looking after Denny, Mrs Morris.'

'Humph. He's a good boy—sometimes.' She then raised her eyebrows at Nana as if asking a silent question. Nana nodded in reply. Mrs Morris scuttled away, across the road.

Denny and Dad went indoors and they stood with Nana in the narrow little passage.

114

'Where's Trisha?' Dad demanded. 'Newport, is it?'

Nana shook her head and pushed open the door of the tiny front room which was seldom used. Denny could hardly believe his eyes. Sitting there, her right arm held up in a scarf, was his mother.

'Mam! *Mam!*' Denny was in the room in one bound, hugging her about the neck until she cried out, laughing, that he'd choke her. Then he stood back and saw that her face was patchy with little cuts and bruises.

'I'm better now, love. Except for my arm. Oh—it's wonderful to see you!'

All this time Dad was standing there without saying a word, but his eyes were a bit shiny.

'Come out to the kitchen with me,' Nana whispered to Denny. 'Your Mam and Dad have to talk—important. We'll bring them a cup of tea in a few minutes.'

In the kitchen, Denny said—'So my Mam was "your friend" in the hospital, Nana.' It was all obvious to Denny now.

'Yes, love. I couldn't tell you. I didn't want to worry you.'

'How did she get hurt?'

'Somebody snatched her handbag, late at night. The work was terrible at that hotel. They can't keep staff. She was on her way home to us when it happened.'

Denny wanted to fight whoever had hurt his Mam. Fight and hurt *them*.

Nana saw his clenched fists. 'I know how you feel, love,' she said. 'But she's safe now.'

'Thank goodness,' said Denny. 'All this goin' away—that's what causes the trouble. Nana . . . it was my dad watching me. Seeing if I was all right. He's been back for ages.'

'I began to guess that, Denny. Roy's a silly boy. Not his fault that he had no work. But he's proud. I understand that. Look—here's your book.' She took it from the sideboard drawer. 'I've had a talk with Sergeant Evans. Told him I thought your Dad was keeping an eye on you.'

Denny was glad to have his book again. Secrets! So many secrets! Nana's tears had been for her Trisha, his Mam. And the words on his birthday card were shaky because his Mam had hurt her writing hand. Rays of light pierced the fog of mystery which had surrounded him for weeks. He made a wry face. They thought he was still a baby! Hiding things from him! Then he thought—aww! they tried to do their best in their own way. He was lucky that they were gathered in under one roof. Stupendous—the way his wish had been granted! His parents *had* come back to him. There as much magic in Owen Street and the muddy old River Taff as there was in all the mountains and lakes of Wales . . .

He heard Nana rattling tea-cups and plates onto a tray.

'Stop grinning or your face will crack,' she said. 'Help me carry this. We'll all have tea in the front room.'

Denny's Dad had removed his boots and was warming his stockinged feet at the gas fire. His Mam, in spite of her injuries, looked younger and less troubled than when she went away.

'In hospital, I had plenty of time to think,' she said. 'I have a lot to be thankful for. Roy, Denny—and you, Mam.'

'You won't make the same old mistakes,' said Nana, pouring tea. 'It isn't going to be easy but we'll all work together. Make a fresh start.'

In that dainty little room with lacy covers on the arms and backs of the easy chairs, Denny thought that he would explode with happiness. But hovering on the outer reaches of that happiness, one thing still bothered him like a small but heavy, inky-dark cloud.

'Dad—what are you building on the riverside?'

Puzzled for a second, Dad said—'Building? Oh—no . . . We're not building anything. We're putting in a retaining wall along the bank—you know—to stop the earth falling. You know about soil erosion?'

'Yes! Yes—I know,' Denny said. 'So you're not *building* at all? Not a hotel—or a factory—or anything?'

'No. We're on a conservation job. The river is silted up badly and it mustn't get worse through landfall.'

Mrs Morris was wrong, then. Denny was warm with contentment. His Dad was helping the river—not polluting it and punishing it just because it was there. For centuries, people had taken it for granted and used it as they pleased—but times were changing, hopefully for the better . . . Now, at least, somebody cared.

'That's great, Dad. Just great.'

They drank tea and munched bara brith—delicious, yeasty, currenty bread. They would probably take hours to catch up on their news and plans but the important matters were settled.

Denny muttered—'Magic Pool, my thanks to you—You made my poem-wish come true!'

'What did you say, love?' Nana asked him.

'Oh—nothin',' said Denny, smiling. Some secrets were not for sharing.

8

After giving enough shocks and surprises to last a lifetime, Fate often has one more trick up her sleeve. Unknown to Denny, there was yet another wonder waiting to happen.

With a double helping of good fortune, when both

his parents returned on the same day, Denny thought that he could not possibly be happier. What more could he want? His world had been topsy-turvy—and had turned the right way up again. He and Mam and Dad were staying at Nana's house until they could find a place of their own. The cosy arrangement was perfect.

Denny went about the house humming tunes from the Magic Pool production, his smile stretching from ear to ear.

'Mmm . . mm . . . mmm . . mmm . . . dee-dum!'

'Somebody's happy!' Nana had turned the front room into a workspace for sewing costumes for the play. Dad had set up her sewing machine near the window for her to see better in the daylight.

First, she measured, pinned and cut into the yards of material supplied by Helen Harris. Then Nana whizzed and whirred away on the machine, feeding in the fabric until amazing costumes emerged from her nimble fingers.

'Stand still, Denny! Oohh—! It's like trying to fit a jumping flea!'

Nana jabbed a line of sharp pins into the red cotton tunic which Denny was trying on over his jeans and jumper. In Denny's story, the tunic was gold. But red fabric was easier to find, Nana said.

'There! That's fine, love.'

'Can I go out now, Nana?' He had not realised that costumes had to be fitted half a dozen times before they looked right. He hopped from one foot to the other, eager to be away to see Jayce.

'Mind the pins!' Nana lifted the tunic over Denny's head.

'Wheww! Is that *it*?'

'Yes, thank you, lovely boy!'

'Nana—I said can I go out?'

Nana twisted around before machining the red material. 'Have you asked your Mam? Don't forget—you do what your Mam tells you now.'

Mam was at the kitchen table, sticking shiny coloured diamonds and circles onto a gold-painted cardboard crown. In hospital, she'd been told not to smoke any more. Her nerves were bad at times but she was being sensible and they were all pleased.

'I'll help you, Mam!'

'Thanks, Den. I've managed most of it. It's amazing what you can do when you try.'

Denny felt a rush of gratitude. With her one good hand, his Mam was helping to make his costume. From a distance, the crown would look like real gold and real jewels. Happily absorbed, they worked together until the last shape was in place. 'We'll show Nana,' Mam said.

Nana was pressing the red tunic. 'Finished! . . . Ooh! what a fabulous crown! Precious jewels! You'll have to keep that one in the Tower of London!'

'Go on, Den—put on the complete costume!' Mam urged him.

Nana was rummaging about in the chaos on the table. 'Here they are. Red tights!'

'*Tights*? *Girls*' tights?' Denny face fell.

'Yes. That's what they wore under those short tunics. Look at the picture!' Nana and Mam were copying the clothes from drawings in the old book of legends.

Denny studied the illustration. Mm. The prince certainly *seemed* to be wearing tights but he insisted—'I could have bare legs—'

'Don't be daft, Denny! You must look the part!' said Nana. 'Go upstairs and get dressed. Here you are—tunic, tights, sandals, belt, bag and crown.' She handed over the items and off Denny went.

In the space of a few minutes, Denny Thomas was transformed into Prince Denzil. He could hardly believe that he was still himself. Before he went downstairs, he practised bowing and waving his arms about in a princely manner. He strode down, stately and dignified, as though descending to the Great Hall of his castle.

There was an impatient knock on the front door, shattering Denny's day-dream.

'I'll get it!' he called to Nana and Mam.

Denny opened the door—Jayce!

'I waited ages for you—' Jayce's words broke off at the sight of Denny in the red and gold prince costume. A smile flickered at the corners of Jayce's mouth. Denny's face blushed as red as his tunic and tights.

Tights! Denny tried to hide his legs behind the open door, bobbing his crowned head at Jayce as he spoke—'Go away! I'll see you later!'

'Don't be stupid. You'll have to be *seen*. No use hidin',' said Jayce, trying to keep a straight face.

'Well . . . you seem to think it's funny or somethin' . . .'

'I don't.' Again, Jayce controlled a smile. 'Brilliant crown!'

'My Mam made it. I helped a bit. Rob Bevan says me an' Ben must have swords so my Dad's making them. Come in, then.'

'I won't laugh at your tights. Promise,' said Jayce.

'Come on, Denny! Let's see you!' called Mam.

The boys went into the front room. 'Ohh! You look marvellous, Den! Doesn't he, Jayce?' Denny's Mam was in raptures.

'That belt could be a little tighter,' Nana pointed out. She notched up the fastening and stood back. 'Lovely!'

'My knees look peculiar,' Denny complained.

'Everybody's knees look peculiar,' Nana told him. 'Knees are made like that. Don't think about them.'

Rat-tat-tat-tapp! Another knock at the door. Emma and her mother came in. Mrs Price walked slowly but she looked happy to be there, involved in the excitement.

Emma's costume was a long green silver gown which Nana had fashioned from floating pieces of shimmering material. Emma's fingernails were painted green and she was to wear a wig of luminous green hair.

They all crammed into the little front room. 'Mega costume, Den!' Emma said, impressed. 'How's your monster outfit gettin' on, Jayce?'

'Nearly ready. Only the fangs to do now.' Jayce's Mam and Dad had made a huge monster head to wear over a body-suit slithery with overlapping grey scales cut out of plastic bin bags. The effect was *gruesome!*

'You'll all look fantastic!' said Denny's Mam.

Rattt-tatt-ttat!

Mrs Morris brought in plates of sandwiches and jam tarts. 'You won't have time to stop sewing today,' she said. 'Shall I put your kettle on?' Soon there was hardly room to move in the clamour of laughing and talking and passing around of tea and food.

Rap-tat-tat-rapp!

Ben and Mrs Sarami rushed in. 'Oh, goodness me! I am not getting Ben's tunic at all right. Can you help me with it, Mrs Lewis, so kind?'

Denny was getting hot and the tights tickled. The three boys moved out into the passage to find some space.

Rapp-ttat-tat-tat!

123

A face peered at them through the letter box and Louise said—'Open the door! I've come for my River-sprite costume!'

Denny opened the door again, saying—'This house has gone crazy!'

When Dad arrived home from work, he brought two wooden swords and gave them to Denny and Ben. Taking one scared look at the crowd, he retreated to the peace of the kitchen. 'The women are loving every minute of this!' he said, laughing. But he was pleased that the boys liked the swords.

Dress Rehearsal was being held that evening at the Community Centre. The public performance of the play was at the Centre on the next evening, Saturday. Rob told them—'Keep to your moves and it will be exactly like acting at the Planet.' All the same, Denny was nervous. The tickets were sold out, programmes printed and there was no escape.

Suddenly—RATT-TATT-TATT-tat-tat-TATT-TATT!

Denny felt more like a doorkeeper than a prince.

'Sorry to barge in!' Rob Bevan said. 'Helen and I knew we'd find most of you here! We can't have Dress Rehearsal at the Centre this evening. We're back at the Planet!'

'I'll make another pot of tea,' said Mrs Morris. 'These old dramatics are thirsty work!'

There were no dressing-rooms at the Planet so the

cast changed into costume in screened-off corners hastily arranged by Rob. Nana put finishing touches to the actors' faces and hair. They whispered to save their voices or sat in silence, mentally going over their lines. The noise and hilarity in Nana's front room seemed to be a world away.

Jayce was a forlorn Monster, certain that he'd spoil the whole play.

'I don't need face-paint to look green,' whispered Emma. 'I feel sick.'

Rob, Helen and the stage crew set out the props and scenery to represent the river bank with the Magic Pool beyond it. Even they spoke in hushed tones. Rob had brought special lighting and he tried out various effects.

Denny wandered off to sit alone near the door. He was pleased with the script adapted from his story. He knew his lines perfectly. There was nothing to do but wait for the Dress Rehearsal to begin. Mr Hopkins came in through the door. He was smartened up for the occasion, wearing a suit which reeked of dry-cleaning, a high-collared shirt and a jazzy tie. His thin strands of hair were plastered down neatly.

At last, Rob called for attention. 'We're ready! Remember: this is a performance! No stopping for any reason at all. If you dry up—forget your lines—Helen will prompt you. Good luck! Go for it!'

The overhead light was switched off. Rob operated the lighting plan, the music began . . . The audience of two—Nana and Mr Hopkins—sat at the far end of the room, waiting for an imaginary curtain to rise.

Denny watched from a screen as the Fishermen rowed their boats and River-sprites dived and swam. Ben—wearing blue tights under his blue tunic—journeyed towards the river, a traveller in a strange land. Ben sang a solo, a lilting, wistful air. Denny saw not a shabby, run-down dance hall but a real river, real mist and a real prince. The scene came alive for him; the Green Lady hovered over the water, beckoning. Then the Monster emerged, roaring and threatening, finally grasping Prince Benjula and dragging him down into the sinister depths of the Magic Pool . . . It was so agonising that Denny wanted to cry out . . . The Fishermen and Sprites mourned the passing of the Prince with a low, eerie melody . . .

Denny walked into the scene . . . but he was not Denny; he *was* Prince Denzil . . . this *was* the River Taff. He was there on the river bank, the mist damp on his face. He spoke to the Fishermen and they shook their heads fearfully, pulling at the oars to hurry their boats away. Gnawing hunger racked him but he did not eat the crust from his bag. His meeting with the Old Hermit came as a relief from his loneliness . . .

Then it was time to move the rock. It was no longer

polystyrene disguised as a boulder. Prince Denzil had to struggle with all his might to move it . . . And there . . . there . . . was the magic ring! It sparkled up at him from a hollow in the ground . . . a ring with a green stone . . . its secret place revealed at last. Denzil had travelled through time, through space, to find it . . . And through those moments of discovery, Prince Denzil was aware that someone, some kindly presence stood outside the circle of light, watching and guiding him . . .

The Green Lady and the Monster were destroyed in spectacular style as the ring did its work. Then all was lightness and joy as the drama ended . . . Denny was back in the Planet again, surrounded by the full cast on stage, with Nana and Mr Hopkins applauding as if they'd never stop.

Something strange and awesome had taken place. Emma handed the ring back to Denny. It was not the ring they used in rehearsals. 'I was sent here to find it,' he thought.

'Are you all right, Denny?' Rob was anxious as he saw Denny sway slightly.

Denny nodded. He was pale, almost stunned. The others were quiet, looking at him. 'May I speak to Nana, please?'

Nana went towards Denny and hugged him. He held out the green-stoned ring to her. 'It was over there, Nana, in a sort of broken bit of floor.'

'Ohh! I don't believe it!' she breathed. 'After all these years' Then she murmured—'Oh . . . my Denzil!' But Denny knew she spoke of another Denzil, his grandfather . . .

Mr Hopkins brought matters back to normal. 'A show an' a' arf, that was! Smashin'! I've seen worse on the telly. Bron—what you got there?'

Nana showed him. 'My engagement ring! I lost it here over forty years ago. It must have dropped down between the floorboards.'

'I remember! We searched high and low for it! Well, I'm blowed!' said Mr Hopkins. The find pleased everybody. It was like a lucky omen for the play.

'I forgot to put our props ring under the stone!' said Helen. 'In fact, I thought the rock was a little too far upstage but there wasn't time to move it.'

Denny thought . . . more magic. Helen forgetting . . . The rock lying over exactly the right spot . . . Strange forces influencing events . . .

Nana was talking to Rob, Helen and Mr Hopkins about her ring. 'Denzil couldn't afford another engagement ring—money was scarce—so all my life I went without one.'

'It fits you perfectly,' said Helen.

'Yes. It fits *now*. It was too loose when we got engaged—but I insisted on wearing it. Of course, it fell off my finger while I was dancing.'

'The Magic Pool brought it back!' said Rob. 'An

amazing coincidence . . . Denny writing his story, the group rehearsing at the Planet . . .'

Coincidence! Loadarubbish! Denny thought. It was *meant* to happen.

Then the topic turned to the Group's performance that evening. Rob, as Director, praised the good work and gave fair criticism where he thought it was needed. Some faces registered disappointment.

'Don't worry!' Helen told them. 'Some Dress Rehearsals are *disasters*! But it always goes right on the night!'

On the way home in the dark, Denny linked arms with Nana. They went past the looming shapes of the church and chapel, past the spooky abandoned shops and houses with their boarded-up windows until they came to the main road where they crossed for Owen Street.

'My lovely boy! You found Nana's ring!'

'I think it wanted to be found, Nana.'

'You're a funny old kid! Oh dear. Poor Jack Truscott!'

'Who?'

'You know. The gentleman who always wears a hat. He lives at the top end of Owen Street.'

'Oh, yeah.' Denny wondered how Mr Hairy Nose came into it.

'You see, Denny, I've never liked Mr Truscott. The night I lost my ring, I saw him pick up something from the dance floor at the Planet and slip it into his pocket. I thought nothing of it until later, when my ring was gone.'

'You thought he kept your ring, Nana?'

'Yes. We were all very poor people. Hardly sixpence between us. He could have sold my ring and made a tidy bit of money . . .'

'But you were wrong.'

'Yes, I was wrong. Poor old Jack. I never told anybody about my suspicions—except for your grandfather. He said I had too much imagination. He wouldn't believe it of Jack. But—stubborn, I am.'

'Well, it's all put right now, Nana.' Another mystery cleared up, Denny thought . . .

'Yes. I shall be extra polite to Mr Truscott when I see him. I misjudged him. Oh—I am ashamed.'

Denny sighed contentedly. 'Never mind, Nana. He never knew. He'll be surprised that you've stopped being snobby, won't he?'

Nana's laugh rang out down the street.

'Come on! It's late! We'll be locked out!'

Hand in hand, no years separating them, they ran towards home.

'The Magic Pool' played to a packed audience at the Community Centre. The performance went off without one fault—well, almost. The Green Lady stood on the Monster's foot but it was a happy accident, causing the biggest monster-roar of the evening!

Everybody was there—the families of the cast and friends old and new ... Mrs Morris and Mr Truscott from Owen Street, Mrs Howells, Pop Lollipop—and Mr Hopkins who liked the show so much that he turned up to see it again.

The programme stated that the script was 'based on a story by Denzil Thomas.' Denny saw Nana put her programme safely in her handbag. She was a great one for keeping things she was proud of. When the curtain-calls were over, there were shouts of 'Author! Author!' Rob said—'Go on, Denny! They're calling for *you*!'

So Denny took a bow all alone. He didn't stay onstage too long, not through shyness but because his tights were sagging—much to Jayce's merriment.

Then Rob played the finale music again and invited the audience to join in the dancing. Nana was first on the stage, her ring twinkling brightly. Mam and Dad danced in the aisle, Mrs Morris and Mr Truscott clapped in time to the music and Mr Hopkins tripped about with Mrs Sarami.

When they left the Centre, the air was mild so nobody hurried home. Denny wasn't often near the river at night. Lights were pin-points in the distance and the water rushed and shushed somewhere below.

Denny's family stood outside the Centre, talking with friends. That afternoon, Denny, Mam and Dad had given Nana a bouquet of flowers. She had pushed her face into the petals and cried with happiness. Mam had sniffed—'D-don't cry, Mam. It's to say 'thank you' for all you do for us.' Then Nana had said how lucky she was to have *them*.

''Night, Emma.' 'Night, Jayce . . .'

''Night!'

'See you tomorrow!'

Emma was happier. A different girl. Her bossy, aggressive manner was put on to hide her dim view of herself. Her lies—and taking the bike—covered a fear that she wasn't as good as other people. She knew better now. She could be a worthwhile person by her own efforts.

And Jayce. Well, he was just—Jayce. Tidy and well-behaved. Scornful of Denny's unrealistic flights of fancy . . . 'As different as chalk and cheese, those two boys!' said Nana. Yet Denny and Jayce were best friends—and probably always would be.

The Taff Stage Group had made new friendships and cemented old ones. There was nothing like working together—meeting failure, solving problems, scoring successes.

Denny turned towards the darkness. He heard the drift of the departing tide, the pull of the undertow. He never tired of the patterns of the river. He thought—'Old Taff—you'll always be here. Whatever happens. You see and hear and know everything.'

The river seemed to say—'Secretsssss . . .'

Denny thought—'Yes. You know all our serious big secrets and our silly little secrets . . . I wonder what you think of us.'

The tide, turning, said, 'Shu-shh . . . Hushhh . . .!'

'Oh—you'll never tell. You with your mud-banks and your hungry birds—you'll always flow in and flow out, never telling.'

The river sped away, pulling out into the Channel, changing . . . 'Like my life,' thought Denny. 'So much has changed—and will change again.' He stood staring at the black glassy retreat of the river.

For the merest second, a pale green glimmer appeared in the distant darkness, out towards the place where Denny had imagined mystery and legend . . . A green glow . . . misty . . . magical . . . Then—nothing. It was gone.

The moonless, starless, cloud-draped sky gave no light but Denny felt at ease there in the gloom. He waited—but the green shining did not appear again.

All at once, he heard a throaty gurgling sound, before a watery fall of silvery amusement. And for ever after, Denny believed without any doubt that he had heard the River Taff laughing.